GABE

M. Tasia

Hope you enjoy Gabe.

M Tasia

www.BOROUGHSPUBLISHINGGROUP.com

PUBLISHER'S NOTE: This is a work of fiction. Names, characters, places and incidents either are the product of the author's imagination or are used fictitiously. Any resemblance to actual events, locales, business establishments or persons, living or dead, is coincidental. Boroughs Publishing Group does not have any control over and does not assume responsibility for author or third-party websites, blogs or critiques or their content.

GABE
Copyright © 2016 M. Tasia

ISBN 978-1537594-16-3

ACKNOWLEDGMENTS

This has only been possible with the love and support of my family. Love you Craig, Samantha and Katie.

Also, wanted to shout out to the talented Virginia and my amazing betas, Paula, Melissa, and Andrea.

GABE

Chapter One

"So…uh…didn't think our morning included hanging off the side of a building…but at least we get out of the staff meeting." Okay, as far as jokes went, that one sucked, but Johnny was beyond freaked and slipping into hysterical very quickly.

Looking around the room at the black, soot-covered faces and only seeing sheer panic staring right back at him didn't help. Johnny knew he was pretty much on his own to come up with a plan. He was no hero by a long shot—truthfully, he was more of a behind-the-scenes kind of guy—but somehow he had to get these three women out of this burning building. They were running out of time; clouds of black smoke rolled upward into the room from the space under the closed door.

"Well, shit. Okay, you three need to find something to stuff under the door to stop that smoke from getting in here," Johnny directed before going over to the lone window and breaking the remaining glass in an attempt to get the attention of the fire department below, praying that none of the glass fell on anyone.

He took a moment to get his first really good look outside and so wished he hadn't. Three stories below was pure chaos. People were running and screaming, and there were police, fire trucks, and EMS vehicles everywhere; their flashing lights reflected off the grey walls. The windows five stories above his head and four over spewed smoke and flames into the cloudless sky.

So screwed, we are so screwed.

"Mr. Jeffrey, what do we do?" Josie clung to his arm and cried, turning her head from side to side, looking for an escape route. He had been mentoring her for weeks while she attended Brighton College. A brilliant, funny young woman intent on turning the world of graphic design "on its ass"—her words, not his. Johnny knew she would, too. He just had to get her out of this damn building first.

He glanced back out the window in time to watch as a beast of a fire truck with a long ladder attached to its back came right up to the front of the building. Firefighters began jumping off even before the truck came to a complete stop.

Please, please, please, God, let that ladder make it up here in time. Okay, brave face time. Brave face? Shit, do I even have a brave face?

"Josie, look at me." Johnny ordered and spoke loudly so the other two women huddled by the open window could hear him over the roar of the fire and sirens. "They just brought out the big guns. That ladder down there on that fire truck is our way out. Maybe we can find you a hot fireman while we're at it." He was trying his best to sound as if everything would be just fine when in truth, he was wondering if a person could survive a drop of three stories. He was not willing to test it out.

"Half of my family are first responders. I could hook you up," Josie responded, wiping away tears and laughing softly. "I haven't heard you talking about a man in your life either." She was desperately trying to act calm, but the panic in her eyes was unmistakeable.

"Just waiting on the right one, Josie." *More like avoiding the wrong ones.*

Johnny continued the "brave face, sound calm" thing and failed miserably, but he had to keep these women focused on rescue and not the alternative. He knew damn well they couldn't go back the way they came. Even with the coats stuffed under the closed door, the smoke was starting to make its way into the room. Johnny noticed that the ladder was being manoeuvred toward the building. In the background, he could make out someone on the ground yelling through a bullhorn for them to stay calm.

Oh yeah, yelling at me to stay calm is really going to make me calm! Seriously?

"It will never reach!" the short blonde from accounting cried. Johnny tried to remember her name, but with everything else going on around him, there wasn't much chance of that happening.

He was about to try and calm her down when they felt the building shudder. It may have only been a tremor, but it was enough to have all four people in the room screaming and clinging together in fear. His heart hopped around his chest like a ping-pong ball.

"I'll never see my baby again! Why did I ever come back from maternity leave early?" Janice sobbed on Josie's shoulder. She had been Johnny's assistant since arriving and was one of the best damn mothers he'd ever had the privilege of knowing. She'd spend every lunch hour at the daycare with Ben and prepared homemade, organic baby foods for him. Her office had a wall of fame showcasing her husband and son. Johnny had no idea why, but the thought of Janice's precious pictures burning to ash was making his stomach churn even harder.

"Yes, you will! You will be there when Ben takes his first steps and every single one after. You got that. We are not giving up!" Johnny had no idea where his courage was coming from, because it was definitely a new development. He had spent the last twenty-nine years of his life under his all-powerful father's thumb—well, at least up until six months ago he did. Johnny had made a clean break from his family once and for all, though "family" was a term he used loosely ever since his beloved mother died while he was still a child. While his father still dogged his every step, Johnny had learned to ignore and misdirect most of his attempts at contact and control. For years he was simply a casualty of his father's ambition. Now that he was free, Johnny prayed he still had a chance to find out who he really was, away from his family's influence.

His father, Dr. Thomas Jeffrey, and his staff were currently somewhere in Asia traveling with his third wife—no, fourth? The man was a slut, plain and simple, but Johnny was thankful his dad had at least waited until after his mom's death. Everything changed in his world when she was taken from them; the pain was suffocating at times. Johnny hadn't seen his older brother in over two years. He'd heard that Dr. Frank Jeffrey, the renowned plastic surgeon to the filthy rich, was currently in Costa Rica yet again, enjoying the hospitality of people with money and power. That had always been his brother's only motivator: power. He took right after the old man.

Johnny was the odd man out, you could say. He had no need for power and enjoyed a comfortable, middle-class life in graphic design, in which he owned Ikea furniture and volunteered at an animal shelter. His mere existence continued to be an embarrassment to his father. Well, that and the fact that Johnny was gay, which he just lumped in with all the other indignities his youngest son had made him endure over the years.

It began with the fact that Johnny didn't quite measure up—literally, he was 5'6" and a hundred and fifty pounds if lucky, compared to his brother's 6'1" and father's 6'3". Oh, he had the same curly blond hair and green eyes as his dear old dad, but where the other two were built like dump trucks, Johnny was all lean muscle from his love of swimming. The fact that he chose to forgo family tradition and not become a doctor was always a great topic of conversation around the holiday table.

"The ladder's getting closer. They're coming to get us." Johnny coughed loudly while trying to speak, holding a ripped piece of the drapes to his mouth. The smoke was really getting thick. He could barely see the far door through the black haze.

"Promise me you won't let me die here!" Janice begged him. "I have to see Ben again. This can't be it!"

The air outside was thick and black, the ground was covered in snaking fire hoses, and shouts rang through the gathered crowd; it felt surreal. The short, blonde-haired woman began to vomit on the floor from her violent coughing. Johnny remembered hearing somewhere that it was the smoke that might kill them first.

Great.

"Janice"—Johnny looked her straight in the eyes so she could see his sincerity—"I swear on my life, I will not leave without you." That was the best he could do, considering he wasn't even sure he was making it out of the building alive, but he would keep those thoughts to himself.

Janice gave him a hopeful smile and stuck her head back out the open window, attempting to get a tiny bit of fresh air. Johnny moved aside to let the three women huddle closer to the window even though they were all slumped on the floor trying to get away from the smoke. He kept hold of their arms as each woman leaned out to get fresh air; he didn't want them getting dizzy and falling out of the window, which of course, with his shitty luck, was exactly what happened.

Josie screamed. Her hands slipped off the ledge and half her body slid out the window. Johnny desperately grabbed at her waist, snagging her belt at the last second, leaving her dangling upside down. Johnny found himself halfway out of the window, desperately holding on to Josie while Janice and the other woman held onto his feet. A few remaining glass shards sliced into his hips. Screams from below echoed off the blackened walls. Johnny held on tight as Josie dangled in midair. Knowing that damn ladder had to be close, he just had to hang on until they reached Josie.

"We got her! Let her go," a deep voice yelled from just below him. Johnny turned his head to see the firefighters on the ladder gently holding Josie to them. *Thank God!*

He released his hold, allowing them to take Josie. The other two women pulled him back inside the window, blood staining the front of his shirt and pants from where the broken shards cut through his clothes and skin. That was when Johnny realized he was getting dizzy. He pushed another flimsy piece of fabric tight against his nose and mouth, but breathing was getting difficult.

"How many people do you have in there?" That same voice echoed into the room. Thank God the firefighters were back.

The women were coughing so badly they couldn't answer, so Johnny inched his way to the window ledge to yell out and noticed the ladder was now only roughly three feet away at most. Hope flared in him; they actually might make it out of this.

"Three now that you have Josie—two women and myself!" Johnny yelled just before another tremor moved through the building.

Screams from the remaining two women were cut short just before he was violently thrown to the ground by an explosion that came from somewhere below them. He turned his head to the right, trying to clear his blurry vision, and saw a leg sticking out from under a large filing cabinet.

Oh, come on!

Johnny crawled on his stomach to the overturned cabinet to find Janice trapped underneath. "Johnny! Johnny, I can't move it. It's too heavy. Please help me!"

"I told you I wouldn't leave without you…" Johnny pushed and pushed, but the damn cabinet moved only a few inches. He had to find something to pry the cabinet up so she could slide out.

As he crawled around the room, he noticed the flames were now licking around the edges of the door. *Time to go!* He turned to where the other woman should be by the open window, but she was gone. Sending up a quick prayer that the firefighter on the ladder had gotten her out, Johnny could do nothing other than continue to look for something to use to pry the cabinet. On the floor, a few feet away from the now flaming door, he saw a steel coat rack. Grabbing it, he raced back to Janice, only registering pain from the heated pole as an afterthought and pushing it aside. He had to get Janice out. He shoved the bar under the cabinet and started pushing. Thankfully the cabinet began to move…and then everything went to hell.

*****

The building was coming down, Gabe knew it. After the last explosion, he and his partner, Lee, were able to grab one of the women huddled by the window and carry her down the ladder. There were two more people in that room, and he would be damned if he'd leave them behind. Seeing his cousin Josie hanging from the window had almost paralyzed him with fear, but thanks to his years of training Gabe didn't miss a beat. He grabbed her out of the air from one of her coworkers who held onto her, saving Josie from a three-story fall headfirst.

Another explosion rocked the back of the building and Gabe raced back up the ladder. He didn't stop at the top. He jumped through the window instead, desperate to find the trapped people. His turnout gear and oxygen tank protected him from the worst of the heat and the thick black smoke that filled the room, obstructing his vision as he scanned for anyone, hoping he wasn't too late.

He heard a loud scraping noise from the back corner. Easing his way closer, he was finally able to make out the same shorter man that saved Josie trying to leverage a filing cabinet off a trapped woman.

"Got the last two, Lee. One trapped," Gabe called into his radio.

"The building's coming down!" Lee answered. "I'm almost at the top of the ladder. Get them out here now!"

Gabe reached the man just as a loud whoosh sounded through the room and flames waved across the ceiling. Time to go. The man with the pole looked up at the flames…but instead of making a run for the window as Gabe had expected, he began to desperately push on the cabinet.

Maybe I'm jaded after all these years.

Gabe grabbed the man's shoulder. The guy cried out in pain before he turned to face him. The smoke was so thick that it was difficult to make out his features, but the burn marks on the guy's shoulder from the steel pole he was using were easy to see.

"You have to get out!" Gabe called. "The ladder is outside the window. GO!"

"No! I won't leave her! She's unconscious. I'll pull her out"—*cough, cough*—"if you can lift this damn thing."

Gabe could tell the man was serious about not leaving without the woman. He figured it must be his wife or someone he loved.

To have someone love you that much... You would never be left behind. He longed for just that.

He put both hands under the edge of the cabinet while the other man dropped the pole and grabbed onto the woman's arms. With one great heave, the cabinet was raised. The man screamed in pain but managed to pull the woman out before falling to the ground himself and coughing violently.

Gabe quickly lifted the woman into his arms and carried her to the window, handing her off to Lee before turning to pick up the last survivor who was still coughing on the floor. Gabe removed his oxygen mask and placed it over the man's face before stepping onto the ladder and heading down to the waiting EMTs. Now that they were away from the smoke, Gabe looked down at the man in his arms to find stunning moss-green eyes staring up at him. *Wow...just wow.*

Desperate for something to clear away the sucker punch that one look had delivered, Gabe could only come up with the other woman in the fire. "Your wife is going to be okay. We got her out thanks to your help."

Gabe gently placed the man down on the waiting gurney. Within moments, one of the EMTs removed the oxygen mask Gabe had given him and replaced it with one from a tank in their rig. Gabe noticed more burns on the man's hands and chest as well as bleeding across his abdomen.

The green-eyed man quickly pushed the mask away from his face. "Wife?"

"Building's clear, Gabe. Now we just need to keep it contained," Lee stated through Gabe's headset.

"Copy, on my way."

"Wife?" the man asked again, looking adorably confused, eyes squinting, leaving a cute little wrinkle between his eyebrows.

"Yes, the lady under the cabinet is already being transported to the hospital," Gabe replied, doing his best to not look into those beautiful eyes or at the tempting bottom lip that was currently between the other man's teeth. The man looked confused for a moment, and then his face lit up in happiness. It was like the clouds parted with just that one look.

Where the hell did that cliché come from?

"Janice! She's safe?"

"Yes, she's on her way to the hospital. You can meet her there when you're transported." Gabe began to back a few feet away; he had to get back to the fire and stop staring at the poor man.

Damn, I've been alone too long when I'm lusting after a married, heterosexual man.

Being a gay firefighter, it wasn't easy for Gabe to find the right partner. Sure, easy sex was always available, but he wanted a commitment. Men might think it was hot to date a fireman, but they soon found the hours he worked and the dangers he faced to be too much, and they would eventually leave.

"Wait, wife? Janice? No...I'm gay. She's my friend—" The man began coughing so violently he was gagging over the side of the gurney.

"We're outta here, Gabe," said Royce, his friend and one of the EMTs, before replacing the oxygen mask.

Gabe ran back over, catching the gurney before it went into the rear of the ambulance. "Wait, what's your name?"

"Johnny Jeffrey."

Gabe and Royce shared a look before Royce gave a slight nod and smiled. Then the doors closed and the ambulance sped away, leaving Gabe and the rest of the firefighters to battle the blaze into the late afternoon. Royce would keep an eye on the guy for Gabe as best he could. After all, the man had saved his young cousin's life, and he couldn't just ignore these intense feelings of attraction, could he?

Chapter Two

Gabe Mason walked out of the showers on his way to his locker on the second floor of the old, brick firehouse that had been a fixture on Main Street in Brighton, Texas since 1895. Gabe loved his job, being a fifth-generation firefighter, and all generations served right here in Brighton. The town was founded on a very simple principle that was as strong today as it was over a hundred years ago: family. Simple term, yes, but sometimes even the simplest terms could be warped by others whose views of what a family should look like differed from your own.

In Brighton, the townspeople embraced all lifestyles and family units. It was a pretty much a live-and-let-live kind of town. In the close-knit community of just over sixty-two hundred people, you knew your neighbors and nothing remained a secret for long—especially with the "White Hair Crew," as they were affectionately nicknamed. One of them was Gabe's very own Grandma Rose, with whom he had a dinner date this evening. After that, he planned on racing over to the hospital to visit Johnny.

Gabe stood staring at himself in the bathroom mirror while he dressed. At thirty-six, he wasn't over the hill by any stretch, but he had laid down some heavy rules for himself years ago. He was tired—tired of being alone and living alone with no one to come home to. His loneliness hung like a lead weight around his neck. But he swore off one-night stands and easy hookups; he'd lost interest in nameless sex long ago. There had been one man over two years ago that Gabe had thought he could spend his life with, but Chris had other plans, leaving one day without so much as a "screw you." Recently he'd been receiving e-mails from Chris every few days—e-mails he immediately deleted. Gabe had no desire to talk to the man after everything that had happened.

At 6'4" and two hundred and forty pounds of muscled fireman, Gabe's attributes always ensured a steady stream of willing partners, but he just wasn't keen on spending his life that way. He wanted a future, a family, a life where he was the focus of someone's love and need. He knew he was dominant; that would never change, and honestly, past lovers could never completely accept his need to be the alpha of the relationship. He had the desire to care for his partner and to be in control, both in and out of the bedroom, and he'd never found anyone to relinquish that control fully to him. Gabe wasn't all dom all the time, but he was the bear of the relationship. His need to hunt, gather, and protect was strong.

For what had to be the fiftieth time that day, the mystery man with those green eyes and curly blond hair drifted through Gabe's mind. Since the fire, he'd felt almost desperate to find Johnny Jeffrey. Gabe had called the hospital and spoke to his cousin, Sam, who worked as an ER nurse. He'd been receiving text updates ever since. Small towns, you had to love them.

So far, Sam reported that Johnny had suffered third-degree burns on his hands, shoulder, and chest and serious damage to his lungs and throat from smoke inhalation. Gabe wasn't sure what chemicals were being stored in the basement of that building, but the smoke was toxic.

"Gabe, Chief wants to see you," Lee yelled from the lunchroom.

"Thanks, Lee. Have a good night," Gabe yelled back before grabbing his bag and heading to the chief's office. Lee had been his teammate for over ten years. They watched each other's backs, and Gabe had even been Lee's best man at his wedding to his partner Frank. Lee and Frank were expecting their first child in the next few weeks. They had found a wonderful gestational surrogate to carry their baby. Gabe had always wanted children and hoped, if he found a partner, they would want children as well. A lot of the men he knew wanted nothing to do with diapers.

The chief was sitting behind a large wooden desk covered in paper, the same desk the chief's dad had used, and his dad before him. One day it would be Gabe's.

"Hey, Dad, what's up?"

"Is it too much to ask for you to call your old man Chief Mason when we're at work?" his dad questioned, not even looking up from his reports.

"Yes, Chief Mason, sir," Gabe responded with a quick salute for good measure.

The chief finally looked at Gabe, perhaps wondering where he went wrong, before he burst out laughing. "Sit down. I hear Josie's been released from the hospital already. Aunt Flo took her home. She's resting with mild smoke inhalation, but she'll be okay."

"Mom left a voice message for me to let me know. That could have gone to hell so easily. One second, I see her leaning out of the window, and the next, she's hanging from the damn thing. I just…I couldn't race up that ladder fast enough to grab her." Gabe shook his head, trying to remove the image of his cousin hanging in midair three stories above the ground. "She would have never survived the fall. Hell, she would have hit her head first." A cold shiver worked its way down Gabe's spine at the thought of Josie falling.

The sound of the rhythmic tick from the plastic clock above the door was the only sound, both men consumed by their own thoughts. The fear of what could have happened was etched in his father's eyes. The chief took a deep breath before he spoke again. "She'll be okay. We'll have to find out the name of that young man who saved her. He was taken to the hospital before I had a chance to ask."

Even though Gabe knew Johnny's name, and had called the hospital to check on him, there was no way in hell he was going to be telling his dad this unless he wanted his whole family swooping in and taking over. "I'll check." *There, that was impersonal enough, right?*

"You on your way to pick your grandmother up for dinner?" The chief gave him an odd look that had Gabe sitting a bit straighter in his seat.

"Yes, but why do I have the feeling you didn't call me in here to talk about Josie or to make sure I picked Grandma Rose up on time?" Gabe had the feeling his mother was involved somehow; his *mom radar* was going nuts.

"You know you're not that young anymore, son, and your mom, she—worries."

If his dad couldn't spit it out, then Gabe knew he was screwed.

"I know Mom wants me to settle down, but I haven't found the right guy yet." *Hope to rectify that very shortly with one green-eyed beauty.*

"How's all that 'not dating' going for you, son? For the last two years since Chris, you've hardly gone on a date or shown any interest in anyone, and your mom is getting desperate. She's calling in *the aunts*." The chief steepled his fingers and leaned forward in his chair.

"No, no way!" Gabe almost flew out of his chair and gave his dad his best you've-got-to-be-shitting-me look. The last time the aunts got involved with one of the nephews' love lives, the U.S. Marshals got involved. "Besides, I met someone." *I hope. Shit! Well, didn't take long to get that out of me, did it?*

Gabe's phone beeped with the text sound he had specifically set for Sam in case something urgent happened to Johnny. He knew he was acting completely out of character but couldn't seem to care. Sure enough, he reached for his phone, unconcerned if his father was offended or not; something could be wrong with Johnny.

Johnny's being admitted. Poor guy's burned pretty badly from that metal pole. They just finished removing the glass and suturing the wounds on his hips and stomach. Ended up with thirty-two stitches. Let you know when I have a room number, cousin.

Gabe simply replied, *Thanks*, and locked his phone. He looked up to find an assessing look on his dad's face.

"I'm sorry, Dad. It was important."

"Was that him, this man you met?" His dad actually looked hopeful. *Does everyone think I'm a lost cause?*

"No, it wasn't him, but it was about him," Gabe answered honestly, but knew his dad wasn't going to give up so easily.

"You know that's not going to work, son, so you might as well get right to the facts or we can beat around the bush and let your mom call in the aunts."

"That's low, old man." His dad simply laughed, leaned back in his chair, and waited. *Damn.* "His name is Johnny Jeffrey. I don't know a lot about him, but I plan on changing that the second he gets out of the hospital, probably sooner."

"The hospital? Is he okay?" His demeanour changed immediately. Everyone thought the fire chief was as tough as they came, but Gabe and his family knew the man was all heart.

"He's the one in that office building fire today, the one who saved Josie. Sam's been keeping me up to date on his condition," Gabe confessed.

"Why didn't you tell me you already found out who he is?" The chief commanded an answer, and Gabe knew he was sunk.

"Because it was more of a personal investigation, not one on behalf of Josie's family."

It took his dad all of two seconds to connect the dots, changing his expression from concern to shock.

"Well, what the hell are you doing here? I'll call your grandmother and let her know you'll reschedule dinner. You go on over there and check in. I'll deal with your mom and the aunts." With that, his dad picked up his cell phone and pointed at the door for Gabe to leave.

His dad was just like him, all alpha. If the man Gabe was interested in was at the hospital, then his dad would make sure no one got in Gabe's way when he wanted to be with that man. His mom was perfect for his dad; she allowed him the control he needed, while in truth, she kept the family and house running. Dad was just along for the ride. The man would move mountains for his wife— just the way it should be, in Gabe's opinion.

Gabe walked out one of the five bays that held the various fire trucks and EMS vehicles. They might be a small town, but they were responsible for four surrounding counties; therefore, they had a large police, fire, and paramedic presence. He threw his bag into the back of his Ford F-250 before climbing in, stopping to take a deep breath. He wondered what he would say to Johnny. Would Johnny want anything to do with him? Did he already have a boyfriend or partner? He hoped not, because Gabe wasn't sure he could back down. He had set his sights on this man and couldn't remember ever feeling this attracted and possessive so soon, not even with Chris. Gabe would just have to work around any obstacles that got in his way. Decision made, he took a second to text Sam to let him know he was on his way.

*****

Johnny imagined this was what the poor people who had asthma felt like; every breath was a struggle and burned his throat and chest. The doctor wanted to keep him on oxygen and observation for the next forty-eight hours. Johnny wasn't entirely sure what he was going to do after that because both of his hands were currently bandaged like a mummy, covering his burns. Hell, even his right shoulder and part of his chest were bandaged, not to mention the multitude of stitches crisscrossing his stomach and hips. He was at a loss on how he would take care of himself. The concerned nurses had asked him for a number of a relative or friend they could call. Considering he was fairly new to this town and wanted nothing to do with his father or brother, he explained politely that there was no one.

His room was dark and he figured he must have fallen asleep. The pain medication they had him on was knocking him on his ass. He heard the rustle of paper and realized he wasn't alone. His heart raced, and Johnny's gut reaction was to panic, assuming his father had somehow found out about the fire and was here. Johnny quickly tried to push himself up into a seated position, but he didn't get far before he was crying out in pain from his burns and stitches.

"Easy, you're safe. Don't move. I'll get what you need, or you'll hurt yourself." Johnny was certain he was dreaming—either that or the drugs were really, really good. There was just no way that the mouth-watering fireman who helped him save Janice and carried him out of the burning building was standing over him, brushing back his hair and gently lowering him down onto the bed. Things like that just didn't happen to someone like him. It had to be the drugs.

"Johnny, you okay? Do you want me to get the nurse?"

Johnny reached out with one bandaged hand to check if he was indeed real, but the sexy fireman gently placed it safely back on the bed. "Careful with your hands. They're covered in burns and blisters. I can't imagine how painful they are."

"You're real? You're here in my room?" Johnny couldn't think of one good reason for Mr. Tall, Dark, and Handsome to be sitting in his room. But, God, he was nice to look at, even if he was a hallucination.

Who was he kidding? The guy was a god, from his confident attitude to his dark brown eyes and black hair cut military short. Hell, he was dressed in a shirt that was valiantly trying to win the battle to contain his muscles.... Johnny would have drooled if his mouth wasn't so damn dry. Unfortunately, his bed was in the way so that was where his perusal ended.

Shoot.

"Yeah, Johnny, I'm real. How are you feeling?"

Johnny was about to answer but realized he didn't even know Mr. Sexy's name.

"What's your name? Or I could just keep calling you Mr. Sexy in my head." If Johnny could have slapped his hand over his mouth, he would have. It had to be the drugs because he definitely said that last part out loud. He could feel his face and ears getting warmer and just knew he was blushing. Okay, smooth he was not.

The fireman smiled and Johnny was sure he saw a tinge of pink crawl up his neck to his ears. "You can call me sexy, but my name is Gabe Mason. Do you remember who I am?"

"You're the fireman who saved us from the building. Thank you for helping me with Janice."—*cough*— "She's been released, they tell me."

"Yes, she was by earlier while you were sleeping and left flowers. Strangely, being pinned to the floor saved your friend from serious smoke inhalation. Her husband will be bringing her and their son by tomorrow to visit with you."

"Ben. He's adorable, but I think it might be a while before I can hold him again." Johnny's throat felt like it had been rubbed raw and he began to cough harder. Between gasps for air, he managed to ask, "Was anyone hurt badly? Josie…someone caught her. Do you know if she's okay?"

Before answering, Gabe brought a straw to Johnny's lips so he could have a sip of water from the cup he held. "No one was fatally injured. Thankfully, we got everyone out in time, but there isn't much left of the building. Josie has been released and is resting at home. Thanks to you, she will be fine. We all owe you for what you did."

"If she and everyone else are fine, I'm good. Wait, what are you doing here?" Johnny could wish all he wanted that there were other reasons for Gabe to be in his room, but why bother dreaming? "Do you have questions about the fire?"

"Nope, I'm here for you, and from what I hear, you're going to need me." Gabe grinned, displaying a pair of dimples that could stop most women and men in their tracks.

"Why?" This was getting stranger by the minute. Johnny stole a quick glance at his IV bag, wondering what the hell he was on. Funny, this only made the handsome man laugh.

"No, you're not hallucinating, though you're on a pretty heavy painkiller. The problem is you have no one listed for your emergency contact or family. Who will be taking care of you when you're released?" The look of concern on Gabe's face was shocking to Johnny; he had no idea why this man would care.

Busted.

"I…ah…I'll be fine." He was not contacting his father. He would try and drag his ass back to the Jeffrey compound where Johnny could be "reconditioned" into a productive part of the family and, of course, less gay.

"No, you won't be. You have third-degree burns, thirty-two stitches and serious smoke inhalation. You won't be able to walk without losing your breath or falling over in pain, let alone care for yourself. You'll be coming home with me. I'll take care of you, and when I'm at the station, my family will help out."

Johnny wondered what alternate universe he had just woken up in where the handsome bear of a man wanted to take him home and care for him while he healed. *Oh, come on! That never happens in reality.* Johnny half expected a big-ass white rabbit with a pocket watch to come running through his room looking for his damn hole. "What…?"

The overhead lights to his room flicked on and the same friendly nurse he remembered from yesterday came walking in. "Good morning boys. Johnny, how are you feeling?"

"Good morning, Nurse Rouse. Johnny's having trouble speaking without straining his throat, so if you don't mind, I'll explain. He's having a lot of pain in his hands and occasional slow, labored breathing while he was sleeping and since waking. He attempted to sit up, but I don't believe he's pulled any stitches." Gabe answered before Johnny even managed to think to catalogue how he was feeling; strangely, Gabe was right. His hands were killing him, he was having a hard time catching his breath, and he prayed he hadn't pulled any stitches.

With that, Gabe Mason took over and Johnny couldn't find a good reason to complain. Gabe wasn't causing him any harm. In fact, if Johnny were honest with himself, he secretly wanted someone to just take control. He knew he was weak for wishing that. His father had physically beaten that into him—never show weakness, always be in control. Would he ever feel comfortable in his own skin? How could he expect to find someone to love him when he didn't love himself that much?

Gabe spoke to Nurse Rouse for several minutes. She looked maternally toward Johnny before leaving to get his medication and new dressings. Gabe turned to Johnny.

"I'll be back in just a few minutes. I have paperwork to fill out and I need to speak with your doctor to set up therapy after your release. Nurse Rouse will be back, but she'll wait until I come back to help with your bandages," Gabe explained before he leaned down and kissed Johnny softly on his forehead.

Johnny was so stunned he could only manage to nod his head in agreement before Gabe left the room. He hadn't a clue how long he sat there just staring off into space before Nurse Rouse came back in chuckling and shaking her head.

"What kind of drugs do you have me on because"—*cough*— "that just didn't happen?" Johnny gasped out, still not able to take complete breaths, but needing answers.

"Now, no more talking. You need to let your lungs and throat heal, doctor's orders. And honestly, I'm not one hundred percent sure what's going on either, but I can tell you I've known that boy and his family all my life. The Masons are good, honest people. His father's the fire chief and Josie's his cousin. But I've never seen Gabe riled up this way, and that's the God's honest truth. I think Dr. Green's head's still spinning." Nurse Rouse laughed before she attached another small bag to his pole and into his IV line. "Just lie back and relax. That pain medication will kick in soon enough and we'll be able to have a look at your burns and those stitches without causing you too much pain. Oh, and don't worry, Gabe's also a trained medic with the fire department, so he'll be able to help you with your medication, bandages, and therapy."

"Why?" Johnny knew he shouldn't speak, but he couldn't understand why this seemingly wonderful man would want to take care of essentially a stranger. His only guess was that maybe this had something to do with helping Josie, and since Gabe was her cousin, Johnny figured he couldn't be crazy, *right?*

"For two reasons—you saved my cousin's life and I'm interested in you."

Neither one of them had noticed that Gabe was back in the room. He went on, "I want to take care of you. If we had met on the street,

I would be pursuing you just the same as I am right now. That's just the way I am. Just because you're injured doesn't change that. It only changes how I go about it." Gabe held a folder and was standing next to a man who looked like an older version of Gabe.

Okay, maybe he's a touch crazy...but why the hell not?

"Okay, but if this is some drug-induced delusion, I'm going to be really pissed when I wake up."

Gabe laughed; it was a deep, full sound that made Johnny's stomach flip. The older man just smiled at Gabe. Johnny coughed again and Nurse Rouse placed a mask over his nose and mouth. The weird vapor made it a bit easier for him to breathe.

"Thank you."

"You're welcome, sweetie. Now, no more talking." Nurse Rouse smiled and began arranging long scissors, gauze, and various other medical supplies on a tray beside the bed. He had a very bad feeling he wasn't going to like this part.

Automatically, his eyes sought out Gabe, who was at his side instantly. "It'll be painful. I'm not going to lie. I will never lie to you. We need to change the bandages regularly to keep your wounds clean. Some of the blisters are breaking and weeping."

Johnny wasn't proud, but the sound he imagined a terrified puppy would make worked its way up his raw throat, and he slammed his eyes shut, not ready to see what his burns looked like just yet. He knew it was bad. The doctor had explained the seriousness of his injuries and likelihood of permanent scarring. Hell, he could feel the intense burning pain, and he really didn't need to see it.

"Easy, babe, I'm right here. I'm not leaving you. Just keep your eyes closed, okay? You don't need to look until you're ready. Listen to my voice and concentrate on that alone."

Without thought, Johnny did exactly what Gabe said to do. He kept his eyes closed tight and listened to this amazing man talk about his family, his crazy aunts and the U.S. Marshals Johnny supposedly saved him from, as well as his grandmother who belonged to a "white hair" group of some kind. He cried out in pain a couple times and Gabe was right there whispering nonsense into his ear, but it was the most meaningful nonsense Johnny had heard since his mother died.

Johnny was getting a little sleepy, he imagined from the pain medication, and began to drift off. He could hear Gabe talking to Nurse Rouse about his stitches, and then the older version of Gabe was giving some sort of directions for something, or perhaps it was a timetable or calendar because it sounded like plans. Johnny was too tired to care, and soon everything just faded away.

Chapter Three

Johnny blinked his sore, dry eyes a few extra times in an attempt to clear his blurry vision, because he sure as shit wasn't seeing what was surrounding him. The last thing he remembered was Gabe's voice calming him while Nurse Rouse changed his bandages, but now he seemed to have fallen down that rabbit hole and ended up in a flower shop. How long had he been asleep and whose flowers were these? He didn't have any close friends and his family would never have spent a dime on something so frivolous unless it happened to be for themselves.

But Johnny had to admit, it did look and smell like heaven in here, even if it all was sent to the wrong room. There were yellow and pink roses, calla lilies, daisies, carnations, and flower arrangements with so many different colorful blooms that he hadn't a clue what they were named. A beautiful sunflower sat proudly in a glass vase beside a row of balloons with various get-well slogans floating happily against the far wall. Another quick scan of the room assured him he was indeed alone and not in the same room from earlier. This one was much bigger and had a window with a view of a park across the street, so close he could make out children playing on a large jungle gym.

This was definitely not his room. His insurance would never even cover the window in this room—heck, his insurance company would have thrown him into the basement if they could get away with it. So how the hell did he end up here? Slowly, he became fully awake and noticed he was hooked up to oxygen and an IV still ran to multiple bags high above him. A clock on the wall flashed 3:19 p.m. He had slept most of the day away.

Then he saw the one thing that put the rest to shame in his eyes; on his side table in a tall, thin silver vase was a single blood-red orchid. Images of his mother slammed into him so quickly he felt light-headed—her beautiful golden hair and gentle blue eyes, sitting with her in her garden. He was tucked safely in her arms while her gorgeous orchids swayed in the wind around them. She would always bring him there when his dad was in one of his moods. Mom would sing loudly and tell him how much she loved him, all in an attempt to drown out the venomous words that spewed from his father's lips.

"You're my beautiful boy, Johnny. You know I love you to the moon." Her soft voice echoed through Johnny's head. *"I'll always love you."*

"Love you to the moon, Momma."

The world was safe for Johnny as long as he was in her arms; he knew this one simple fact from a very young age. Then she was taken away from him. The only love and light in his life was gone because some person decided to get high and drive. A young Johnny was left alone with the man who viewed him as a failure—he was too soft and too small to be a proper Jeffrey—and decided to set about correcting what nature had somehow screwed up—painfully.

The orchid was stunning and made Johnny feel that same love and safety from so many years ago. For one brief moment, he wished someone had actually sent it to him—because this was still not his room. Johnny had heard of mix-ups in overcrowded hospitals of course but never actually thought he would become one. Brighton didn't strike him as an "overcrowded" town, which was another reason Johnny had moved here. He needed peace. After all the years trapped trying to please his tyrant of a father, Johnny craved peace and acceptance.

Carefully, Johnny turned his head, trying not to pull on his burned shoulder too badly, but he was in desperate need of a drink to soothe his raw throat. Then, of course, reality came crashing in, reminding Johnny that he couldn't move his mummified hands, let alone pour himself a glass of water or even hold the damn thing.

Well, this should be interesting. Let it not be said that Johnny Jeffrey just gives up.

Johnny oh-so slowly pushed himself up into a sitting position using his elbows. His hands burned and his stitches pulled, but he proudly sat and reached over for the entire pitcher of water. He knew he couldn't wrap his hands around the smaller cup but the pitcher was at least three times the size, so he was able to lift it easily, even if painfully. Without a straw, Johnny had no other choice but to tip the jug back and drink from the spout, not exactly classy, but he was so thirsty he didn't care at this point.

The cool water felt painful against his dry, sore throat but all was going well—at least up until the door to his room opened and a small sprite of a woman with blonde hair and big blue eyes strode in. She carried multiple bags and another bouquet of flowers. Johnny was so caught off guard that the hold he had on the pitcher began to slip. Tsking, the woman dropped her load and rushed over. Smiling widely, she held the bottom of the pitcher in her hands so that Johnny could finish drinking.

"Dear, you should have called the nurse for help. I just stepped out for a moment to call home and pick up these bags from the car." The sweet, crazy lady rushed around Johnny, bringing the nurses' call button closer to his side and raising the bed so he could lean back. She even went as far as tucking him back in.

"Thank you...but I think you might be in the wrong room, or maybe I'm in the wrong room because I'm sure none of this is for me." Johnny gestured toward all the flowers, as if the mystery lady could somehow have missed the garden surrounding her.

"No, Johnny, this is your room, and I'm here to see you, sweetheart. Actually, you've had a few visitors, but you've been fast asleep since early this morning, according to Gabe. It's best you rest as much as you can anyway so that you can start to heal."

"I'm sorry...do you know Gabe?" Johnny gasped, his lungs burning with the effort it took him to talk.

"Gabe said you weren't supposed to be talking and exerting your lungs, so how about I explain everything, dear, and you just get comfortable."

Johnny figured he might as well hear her out because he was pretty much trapped in the bed at her mercy anyway. The little spitfire raced around the room adjusting the drapes and his bedding...again. She put a straw in the pitcher of water and pushed it close to the side of his bed, and then finally picked up her bags, depositing them on his dresser before gliding into the chair beside his bed. Johnny liked her immediately but was exhausted from just watching her. She looked to be in her late fifties, but she hustled around his room with the energy of a twenty-year-old.

"I'm Ellen Mason, Gabe's mom. You can call me Mom," she happily explained. "Gabe has been called in to cover a fire over at the Jaspers' farm. Seems one of their hay barns went up, and with all this dry weather we've been having, they're afraid it could catch to the nearby fields. Trust me when I tell you he didn't want to leave you, but this is the life of a firefighter, dear. That's when family comes in handy. I'm sure he'll be putting in for some time off now that he'll be helping you heal."

Mom? That was the only word he caught in that whole explanation. He hadn't used that particular word in a very long time, and strangely, he felt a warmth spread inside him.

"I don't understand." Johnny had to admit it was nice having someone care about him, but he still wasn't sure what to make of this whole situation.

"That's okay, Johnny. Just know that you have the Mason family to back you up, even though Gabe's banned everyone but me and his father from the hospital—something about not wanting to scare you off with all of us hovering at once. But we'll see how many we can sneak in before he catches on." Ellen gave Johnny a conspiratorial wink before digging into her bags. The more time he spent with Ellen, the more Johnny liked her. She seemed to be tough and gentle at the same time with a huge dose of mischief sprinkled in. He bet Ellen gave Gabe's dad a run for his money.

Johnny was curious now: Exactly how big was Gabe's family that he wanted them to steer clear of the hospital?

"How big is the family?"

"Oh, Johnny, honey, I'm going to have to draw you a chart on that because there's just no way you could remember them all. Let's see, to make it simple, I'll start with the immediate family in the area. Gabe's father, Roger, has three brothers and one sister, so Gabe has three uncles, four aunts, three younger sisters, two brothers-in-law, fourteen cousins, a niece, nephew, and Roger's mother, Grandma Rose." Ellen must have seen the panic in Johnny's eyes because she quickly added, "Don't worry, they won't visit all at once. I think."

That...that's roughly thirty! Oh shit! That's a lot of freaking people. And that was only the immediate family in the area? Leave it to me to find a cult, a very helpful cult, but still a damn cult.

"Johnny, you look a bit pale. Here, I brought you some of my famous chicken casserole, cut up in nice small pieces so not to hurt your throat. Hospital food will not be enough to get you healthy again." With that, Ellen pulled a plastic container from one of the bags. Honestly, Johnny was starving and the casserole looked amazing, but he just couldn't figure out how he would get the food into his mouth.

But instead of asking the obvious question, Johnny was still nervous about the room and the flowers. It would break him to pay for all this. "Ellen, how did I end up in a bigger room? My insurance isn't going to cover this, and the flowers"—*cough*—"who…?"

Ellen quickly moved his pitcher of water even closer so that Johnny could lean into the straw and take a much-needed drink before she began to explain. "You don't have to worry about the room, dear. Whatever your insurance doesn't cover will be seen to. As for the flowers, well, between family and friends, they've been arriving all day."

"But—," Johnny began but was quickly cut off by one look from Ellen.

"No buts, young man. You will not worry about the room and you will accept the gifts you've been given because you deserve them, and I will not hear another word on it." It quickly became apparent to Johnny that Mrs. Ellen Mason had dealt with men much larger than himself and had the steel backbone to prove it.

Therefore, Johnny gave the only acceptable answer. "Yes, ma'am."

Ellen laughed softly and smiled. "I knew you and I would get along. Took me years to get the men of this family in line, but you caught on right off."

Johnny also knew in that moment that they would get along just fine as well, and perhaps they weren't in a cult after all. But still, he needed to know who sent the red orchid closest to him. He decided against talking any longer and simply pointed toward the beautiful bloom.

Ellen caught on quickly to Johnny's attempt at charades. "Do you wish to know who brought that one?"

"Yes, please. It's important," Johnny replied, forgetting his decision not to speak, as he mentally rifled through everyone he might know who would remember his mother's garden. No one other than his father and brother came to mind. The flowerbeds had been bulldozed within a week of her death, replaced by a shiny new garage to store all of his father's vintage cars.

"This is from Gabe, dear. Actually, it's from the greenhouse he has in his backyard." Ellen answered with a great deal of pride. "Do you like orchids, Johnny?"

"My mother's favorite," Johnny gasped, deciding right there he really needed to get a handle on not talking for the time being. Picturing the hulking firefighter tending flowers in his greenhouse shouldn't have given Johnny this much joy, but it did. He wondered if Gabe would permit him to visit his greenhouse someday, maybe allow him to spend time sitting with the orchids for just a little while.

"Johnny, do you want me to call your mother to let her know what's happened?"

"Died…long ago."

"Oh, I'm so sorry, Johnny. And your father?"

Johnny simply shook his head, not wanting to open that painful door. Instead, he took renewed interest in his dinner, still trying to figure out how to get it from the container and into his mouth. Unlike the water, he couldn't simply pour it. Looking back toward Ellen, he noticed the sympathy flash in her eyes, but she quickly masked it with her normal enthusiasm.

"You've got to be hungry. Let's get you fed." Ellen retrieved silverware from her bags before turning toward Johnny. "Now, young man, you are about to have a real treat. This is my mom's recipe and, if I do say so myself, it's the best in the county, and don't you let Gabe's aunts tell you otherwise. They're just jealous." Johnny could tell each word she spoke about her family was laced with love, bringing home just how lonely Johnny really was.

He decided then and there he would accept the care of these fine people for the time he was allowed and soak up as much of these feelings as he could. That way, when he went back to his own solitary life, Johnny could pull on these memories to get him through.

Ironically, Ellen took over much like her son. It was quickly becoming a theme. Considering Johnny couldn't do anything for himself, he appreciated each and every gesture. She spoon-fed him the best damn chicken casserole he had ever tasted. When a young male nurse named Sam popped his head into Johnny's room, giving it a quick scan before strolling in, it seemed odd at the time. It wasn't until Johnny was informed that Sam was Gabe's cousin and he had chosen to ignore Gabe's decree to stay away from Johnny's room, considering he worked at the hospital, that Johnny understood the spy routine. Johnny was pretty sure that this would be a common occurrence amongst the Mason family members.

Sam, with the help of another young nurse named Amanda, checked all of Johnny's vitals and dressings, replaced a bag on his IV, and, much to his embarrassment, helped him into the bathroom and with his sponge bath. Through the entire humiliating ordeal, they repeatedly assured Johnny that this was nothing to be concerned about, that they were nurses and he was family after all.

Finally cleaned, fed, and medicated, Johnny was back in his bed and ready for a nap. Sam booked it out of the room once Ellen received a call from the chief to let her know that he and Gabe had made it back safely and should be at the hospital within the hour. Johnny knew the call was a warning from Ellen's husband to have everyone out of the room before Gabe arrived, but Ellen simply tutted into the phone before she hung up.

"Honestly, you would think my husband and son didn't know me at all. Of course there will be family sneaking in and out. What did they expect?" Ellen smiled before she placed her tiny hand on Johnny's uninjured shoulder and turned back to the television, which someone had rolled in while he was in the bathroom. Johnny snuggled further into the cocoon of pillows Ellen had amassed, while she got comfortable in a reclining chair beside the bed. They both went back to a movie starring Hugh Jackman and his muscles; thirty minutes later, Johnny and Ellen were both entranced.

"Do we even care what the plot line of this movie is?" Johnny finally asked after Hugh's fine ass flexed across the screen for a second time.

"Not a damn clue, but I can't look away," admitted Ellen without breaking eye contact with the screen.

"He has a phenomenal ass, I'll give him that," Johnny commented.

"Agreed," Ellen replied.

"Who has a phenomenal ass?" a deep voice asked, causing both Johnny and Ellen to squeal in fright. The water bottle Ellen was holding went flying across the room and into a bright green balloon, popping it.

Johnny looked up to see Gabe and the chief standing just inside the door, trying to contain their laughter, until the chief finally broke down and laughed outright.

"Roger Mason, how dare you sneak up on a person like that? You could have scared Johnny," Ellen admonished, but by the deep shade of red covering her face and ears, Johnny was pretty confident this had nothing to do with him.

"Don't drag me into this. I can't help it if your husband caught you ogling another man's ass." Johnny spoke softly through his own muted laughter at how flustered Ellen had become by this point.

"You were looking at that same ass, young man," Ellen shot while Gabe came around to the other side of the bed and brushed a stray blond curl away from Johnny's face.

"I can look all I want, *Mom.* Besides, you put the movie on." Johnny raised his bandaged hands and smirked like the little shit he was.

"Oh, now you call me Mom when we're busted." Ellen threw her hands in the air in mock surrender.

"I can see this may not have been such a good plan," the chief grumbled good-naturedly. "They seem like two of a kind, son. That can't be good for my blood pressure."

"I'm beginning to wonder that myself," Gabe laughed. "You look better, Johnny. How are you feeling, babe?"

"Better, thank you." He paused to cough. "Mom's taken very good care of me." Johnny was having a hard time dragging his eyes away from Gabe. He was like a damn magnet and Johnny was stuck. It could have been his chiselled features, his commanding presence, or the fact that he was drop-dead gorgeous, but in truth, it was Gabe's eyes. They were so dark and filled with concern, compassion, and something Johnny hadn't seen directed toward him in a long time—affection.

"Well, I can see you have everything under control here, son," Chief Mason commented as Ellen began to gather her bags getting ready to leave with her husband. The chief stepped forward with his hand out. "We weren't introduced before. I'm Chief Roger Mason, Gabe's father."

Johnny looked at the chief's outstretched hand for a moment before he lifted his bandaged hands into the air. Chief Mason's eyes went from welcoming to stricken in seconds.

"Ah, damn, I'm sorry, Johnny. I didn't even think."

"No worries." Johnny sighed before moving his hands aside. "It's nice to meet you, Chief Mason."

"Dad."

"Sorry…?"

"You can't play favorites, Johnny. If Ellen gets 'Mom,' I get 'Dad.'"

"Wha—?"

"Well, gotta go. I'll see you tomorrow, Johnny." Ellen rushed over and kissed both Johnny and Gabe on their respective cheeks. "I'll call you later, Gabe." In a flourish of bags, Ellen flew out of the door with a smiling chief in tow.

"Please believe me—my family is actually sane, although that may be hard to accept at the moment," Gabe confessed while they both sat staring at the closed door.

"Have you consulted a professional about that?" Johnny deadpanned.

"Uncle Henry's a psychiatrist…but he might be biased," Gabe answered, a huge smile showcasing those deep dimples set in the dark stubble covering his cheeks. Johnny knew he was lost if he spent any time with this man.

Does Gabe even know he's walking among us mere mortals? I don't stand a chance; this can never work out. I have to keep my distance. I can't let this destroy me when I inevitably fall for him.

Chapter Four

By the next morning, Johnny knew something was seriously wrong—well, more wrong than all his current injuries. At Johnny's urging, Gabe had finally left late last evening so he could get a decent night's sleep in his own bed after spending the day fighting a fire. Now Johnny wished he'd never said a word; then Gabe would be with him as everything turned into mayhem around him. Just after 4:00 a.m., Johnny woke gasping for breath. He felt like he was drowning. Every time he coughed, he brought up a disgusting, frothy, pink phlegm of some kind. All in all, he was beginning to panic.

After several X-rays, an ultrasound of his lungs, and blood and oxygen saturation tests, a respiratory specialist was called in to consult and Johnny was diagnosed with acute noncardiogenic pulmonary edema. It was caused not only by the damage from all the smoke he inhaled, but also by the chemicals in that smoke. He didn't care what the hell it was or why he had it. Johnny just wanted someone to fix it now. He heard someone say something about a membrane, air sacs, and capillaries, but what it all came down to was the fact that fluid was filling his right lung and his body was battling to get enough oxygen.

More bags of clear liquid were attached to his IV line as nurses rushed in and out of his room. Nurse Rouse was at his side checking machines, her hand flying across her clipboard. She tried to look calm, but the pinched lines around her eyes and lips gave her away. Something was seriously wrong.

"I've called Gabe, Johnny. He's on his way. Don't worry."

She tried reassuring him, but her continued monitoring of equipment and rigid stance confirmed she was worrying enough for both of them. *Great, just great. I'm finally building a life with a new job and home only to almost die in a fire, possibly lose the use of my hands and by extension my career, and now something else is going wrong. Perfect! And I didn't even get to play with the hot fireman.*

Okay, not the best time to whine about that one.

Every minute that passed, Johnny struggled a bit harder to breathe. His eyesight was beginning to get blurry. As teardrops of light filtered through, Nurse Rouse began yelling, but it seemed to be happening from so far away.

"Dr. Green! He's losing consciousness and his oxygen saturation levels are dropping!"

"Prepare to intubate. We have to secure his airway," Dr. Green ordered and people began to run. Or at least Johnny thought that's what they were doing, but really it was all just a blur.

Johnny felt detached from the entire scene, as if he were weightless, simply watching but not involved. He knew he should be terrified, perhaps he even looked it, but really all he wanted was a nap. He was so tired. Machines were wheeled in and Johnny's bed was lowered. By now, he was full-on hyperventilating, dragging each and every breath in through what felt like mud.

Nurse Rouse put a syringe to a port on his IV line before giving Johnny a troubled smile. "You sleep now, Johnny. You'll be just fine."

The last thing he remembered were machines ringing, shouts from a vaguely familiar voice, and Dr. Green's face above him before everything went black.

*****

Johnny had been on the ventilator for almost two days, and Gabe had no intention of leaving him again, whether Johnny was conscious or not. At the moment he was being kept sedated to give his injured lungs a chance to heal as various medicines were administered through either his tracheal tube or IV. Also, waking up attached to a machine wasn't something anyone wanted Johnny to experience; he'd been through enough. Gabe had raced into Johnny's room as he was being sedated. The fear he saw on Johnny's face sent acid clawing up his throat. It was something he never wanted to experience again. Nurse Rouse assured him that Johnny wasn't fully conscious at that moment and would likely not remember what occurred; he hoped she was right.

The dark, empty halls were a reminder of just how late it was in the evening of the second day of his vigil. Gabe felt drained and exhausted, but he had to stay strong for Johnny; he would need him when he woke up. So there he sat reading an old horror novel out loud so Johnny would know he wasn't alone. Earlier in the day, they read the *Brighton Bugler* together. There were plenty of studies proving that unconscious people could sometimes hear what was happening around them, and if Johnny could, Gabe was determined to make sure he knew he was safe and that Gabe was there watching over him.

His mother and father had been by often, bringing food and clean clothes or just sitting and keeping him company. But honestly, all he needed was for Johnny to heal and open those clear green eyes of his. Gabe would wait right here until that happened. The remainder of the family were calling for updates but stayed away, not wishing to add the stress of a strange group of people to Johnny's recovery.

"Okay, we are never burying our pets in some messed-up cemetery. I think we'll stay with the mysteries from now on if you don't mind, or else I'll be having nightmares." Gabe laughed softly, and placed the now closed book on the small side table. He gently held on to Johnny's arm just above his bandaged hands. Fresh orchids from his garden sat closest to the bed. Gabe's mother had stopped by his greenhouse. The sweet scent of jasmine softly lingered in the air. "I pray you can hear me or even feel my touch and know you're not alone. I'll never be far away, baby. You only need to worry about getting better. Once you heal up I want to share so much with you."

Gabe knew his emotions were all over the place and took several deep breaths to calm the hell down. "You see, I'll tell you a secret. I'm not a safe bet for you, Johnny. Things have happened, things I can't change but have changed me. And the only reason I'm brave enough to tell you this now is because you're unconscious. I find it hard to trust people. I'm stubborn and bossy, and I need to be needed, if that even makes sense." Gabe rubbed the palm of his hand across the back of his neck before he continued. "There's just something about you. I've been drawn to you since the first time I saw you trying to lift that cabinet off your co-worker. My instincts tell me we could have something special, and if you let me, I promise to try my damnedest to give this my all."

Gabe sat for a few moments just running his hand up and down Johnny's pale arm, hoping that one day he would feel those same arms holding him tight. He just needed to concentrate on making that happen and not on any other possible outcomes.

"So this is where I find you." An all too familiar voice broke Gabe's peace. He clenched his teeth, enraged by the very thought of Chris anywhere near Johnny.

"How did you get in here? This is a critical-care floor. How did you even know where to find me?" Gabe tenderly tucked Johnny's arm back under his blanket before rounding the bed and closing in fast on his ex-fiancé.

The smug smile on Chris's face was quickly replaced by fear as his hands flew up in surrender. "When you didn't come home after a couple days I followed your mom here. I just wanted to talk, sweetheart."

"Talk... *What?* Who the hell do you think you are coming here after what you did to me?" Gabe grabbed Chris by his shirt and dragged him out of the room away from Johnny and to the nurses' station. He wanted a peaceful environment around Johnny so he could heal and feel safe. Chris was not going to ruin that.

Nurse Moore took one look at them and jumped into action. "Call security. This man isn't supposed to be on this ward." She, along with many in the community, knew Chris's history and the events of two years ago.

"Wait, wait! I just wanted to talk, Gabe. Can't you give me five minutes?" Chris snaked his hand up Gabe's chest and around his neck. "Come on, honey, you know you missed me."

Waving a red cape in front of a rampaging bull is insanity; those last words might as well have been flashing crimson for the effect it was having on Gabe. "Missed you?" Gabe grabbed Chris's hands and tore them from around his neck, repulsed by his touch.

"Yeah, we had some good times together, Gabe." Chris's voice carried across the room and held enough innuendo that no one was left wondering what exactly he was referring to.

"Miss what exactly? The lies, the theft, the embarrassment, the pain, the anger? What exactly was I supposed to have missed?" Gabe's voice came out calm though he was raging on the inside. All he knew was that this vile man needed to be away from Johnny now. "Leave now or be carried out."

Gabe pointed to the three security guards standing behind Chris; one was already holding his handcuffs at the ready. Chris took an appraising look around. Gabe imagined he was deciding whether or not he should leave without screaming the walls down. *How could I have ever found this man attractive? Sure, physically he's tall, blond, and handsome, but how did I miss the sickness inside him? Those same blue eyes that used to make me smile almost seem cruel.*

"Fine, I'll go, but we aren't finished, Gabe." Chris looked like a petulant child with his hands on his hips and nose in the air.

Yep, no idea what I saw in him.

Gabe simply shook his head as the three guards led Chris away. "I don't want him able to get back in here."

"Don't worry; now that we know, we can keep an eye out for him. I'll inform the staff that he's been warned. If he tries again, we'll call the police," Dr. Green stated as he joined their small group. Though the doctor had moved to Brighton just under one year ago, he had been a perfect fit in the small community. "Now that the excitement's over, let's go check in with Johnny and see how he's progressing."

"Yes, I didn't want to leave him alone, but I had to get Chris out of his room," Gabe agreed.

"Understandable." The doctor's pale eyes looked tired but determined. "Johnny's improving every day, Gabe. Soon we'll have him breathing again on his own."

"Thanks, Doc." Gabe resumed his position at Johnny's bedside. Johnny's body looked so small in the middle of the crisp, white bedding. The melody of beeps and bells became background noise once the doctor began examining Johnny.

Twenty tense minutes later, Dr. Green confirmed yet again that Johnny was definitely recovering. If all went to plan, he would be able to remove the breathing tube within the next twenty-four hours. Once that was done, he would reverse Johnny's sedation, allowing him to regain consciousness over the following days. Soon Gabe and Johnny were alone once again. Gabe managed to get a baseball game on the circa-1980s wood-grained, plastic-encased beast in the corner. He pulled his reclining chair over beside the bed, wrapped his arm around Johnny's, and began to explain how the Brighton Bulldogs made it all the way to the five counties finals last year and how Gabe would be sharing his season tickets with Johnny.

*****

The deep timbre of a voice Johnny recognized flowed through him thick and heavy, pulling Johnny forward before the connection sliced clean away. If he tried to concentrate, the words would simply vanish even faster. The only time the familiar voice stayed long enough to make out what was being said was when he relaxed and let the sound cover him like a warm blanket. *Gabe.* The nothingness of the words meant everything to him. Gabe was here. He hadn't left; that was all that mattered to him.

Johnny swore there had to be sand embedded in his eyes and his throat was on fire, but he could breathe—not deeply but without too much pain. At least his mouth was empty now, no longer filled with what he remembered felt like hard plastic. Now he just needed to open his eyes to see Gabe, but they outright refused to move. The more he struggled, the more exhausted he became until sleep finally took him again. This routine replayed itself too many times to count, and Johnny had just about enough of this torment. He was determined to open his eyes this time.

Johnny reached out with his bandaged hands, searching for that sweet man who was humming softly in his ear, calming Johnny with his strength and reassurance. But Johnny didn't want calm right now. He wanted to be awake. He wanted Gabe. Thrashing harder against what had to be a chest, Johnny finally felt the dry scrape of his eyelids opening, and light poured in, blinding him.

"Li...t," he managed to push out as tears ran streaming down his face.

"Turn down the light. Hold on, baby. This will help." The wet cloth that covered his still tearing eyes felt like heaven. "Johnny, I'm going to bring a cup to your lips so you can have a small drink of water."

Oh God, yes, water please.

He felt the hard plastic being pressed to his dry lips, thankful for the fact that there wasn't a straw involved. At the moment, he wasn't sure he had enough strength to breathe properly let alone suck up water. The liquid cooled and wet his parched mouth, but the moment it reached his damaged throat, he began to gag. He was positive razor blades would have been easier to swallow. While a small amount stayed down, the rest was caught by another towel held to his chin by Ellen—*Mom*.

The wet cloth that had been protecting his sensitive eyes had been removed and, mercifully, the only light in the room came from the open window. The strong, handsome face of the man he'd been listening to in the darkness hovered over him smiling, showing off those sexy dimples of his.

"You're finally awake." Gabe's eyes filled with tears as he sucked in a deep breath. Even with his blurry vision, Johnny could see the tension melting away, leaving a happy, exhausted man in its place.

"Hi," Johnny managed in a rough, raspy voice that reminded him of a rusted hinge being torn open. It sounded painful, which was fitting considering it hurt like hell.

"Shhh, don't stress your throat, Johnny. Just rest." Gabe leaned down and kissed Johnny on his cheek. His eyes sparkled, even if they were surrounded by dark circles. "Is Dr. Green on his way, Mom?"

"Yes, dear," Ellen answered, still clutching the towel as her own eyes filled. "The nurse ran to get him. They shouldn't be long, son. Johnny, we're so happy to finally have you back, young man." She turned and sniffled all the way to the bathroom, where Johnny was confident she was taking a few minutes to pull herself together.

The only problem was, Johnny had no idea why everyone was acting this way.

Why is Ellen crying? Why does Gabe look exhausted? Why am I in a different room again? Shit, what's going on?

"What happened?"

Gabe cupped the side of Johnny's face with his large, calloused hand. Johnny leaned into the gentle touch, needing to feel him close. Something had changed.

"You've been unconscious and on a ventilator for three days, Johnny. God, I've never felt so helpless. They removed your breathing tube yesterday afternoon. Dr. Green and the nurses have been taking good care of you."

"I remember your voice... right? You d-didn't leave me." Johnny spoke softly, trying not to hurt his throat more than it already had been, but he needed to know if what he remembered was real or if he had imagined the whole thing. The warmth he felt when looking at Gabe only confirmed the man had managed to slip into Johnny's heart somehow, but that was impossible. They'd only met days ago and it sounded as if Johnny had been unconscious for most of it.

"No, I would never leave you, baby." Gabe brushed Johnny's hair away from his face and carefully tucked the covers around Johnny's body. The bedding looked dishevelled from his thrashing, but thankfully Gabe had been able to restrain him enough so that he didn't accidentally pull his IV line out of his arm or the oxygen tube from his nose. "I'll explain everything soon, but you need to promise me not to stress your lungs by talking. All you need to do is concentrate on healing. I never want to see you that sick ever again." Gabe's voice cracked slightly. This strong, brave man who spent his entire life saving others broke down at the thought of Johnny's suffering, and seeing that did something to Johnny. Johnny would have to examine that change later, when his head stopped spinning.

"Me either," Johnny agreed. Even though he still had no idea what had happened, the relief in Gabe's eyes was enough to confirm that his condition must have been grave.

Gabe slowly leaned down, bringing his face mere inches away from Johnny's. His eyes, the color of dark chocolate, seemed to glow from within. His soft lips lowered to caress Johnny's, tender and slow, with the light dance of his tongue against Johnny's lips. The moment was over way too quickly for Johnny's liking.

"I see our patient is awake," Dr. Green announced from the doorway and smiled wide before entering with a nurse. "How are you feeling, Johnny?"

"Sore… weak," Johnny answered, but ran out of breath again before he could continue.

"Okay, I'm going to ask you some questions and I want you to just nod your head yes or no," the doctor instructed while he placed his stethoscope in his ears. "Gabe, can you help Johnny sit up so I can listen to his lungs?"

Gabe slipped his arms behind Johnny's back and cradled him, slowly lifting Johnny until he was sitting upright in the bed. Dr. Green listened to Johnny's chest and back. Johnny wasn't sure what the doctor was listening for, but he was glad the man didn't ask him to breathe deeply or anything. He was pretty sure it would be a while before that happened, considering it felt like he had a truck parked on his chest. Mom came back out of the bathroom with her cell phone against her ear, smiling like a loon. Johnny was still struck by the fact that this family so easily accepted him into their fold.

The doctor continued with his questions and examination. Johnny concentrated on Gabe and not his discomfort as the gentle man kept hold of him. He could feel the flex and bunch of hard muscle under Gabe's shirt. After several minutes, Gabe was asked to lower him back onto the bed, but Johnny held onto Gabe's shirt for a few extra seconds, not ready to let him go just yet. Johnny didn't know why he was behaving this way, but no one seemed to mind as Gabe rubbed his cheek against Johnny's head and simply held him. Gabe let go after a few moments and moved only a couple feet back to allow the nurse to check his blood pressure and oxygen levels.

"Your lungs sound much better, Johnny," said Dr. Green. "They're healing nicely, but it will take a while before you're even cleared to leave the hospital."

"That bad?" Johnny asked.

"Yes, it was very serious. I don't think now's the time to discuss everything that's happened, considering you just regained consciousness and are still feeling the effects of being sedated. We'll give you some time to get your bearings back."

"Thank y-you," Johnny gasped, and agreed talking would have to wait until he could at least take a decent breath in.

"You're welcome." Dr. Green gathered a folder from the side table, bringing Johnny's attention to the bouquet of orchids in a clay vase beside his bed.

He looked up to see Gabe watching him closely. Johnny reached out to touch the beautiful pink petals but remembered his bandages at the last moment and pulled his hand back. Gabe immediately moved the vase to the edge of the small table so that it was closer to Johnny, making him smile.

"Gabe, can I talk to you for a moment?" Dr. Green asked before heading toward the door.

"Yes, I'll be right out," Gabe answered. "Just rest, honey. Mom's right here with you. When I get back, we'll get you cleaned up and comfortable."

Gabe followed the doctor out of the room and Ellen took his place at Johnny's side. "Here, Johnny, have another sip of water, dear. It'll be easier to keep down this time." He gave her an unconvinced look but obediently leaned forward toward the cup she held. The cool liquid did stay down this time and only burned his throat a little. "There you go. We'll keep up on the fluids until we can get some broth into you."

"Thank you, Mom." Johnny tried desperately to prevent his tears from falling, but there was nothing he could do to stop them. Quickly, he turned his face away from Ellen as the events of the last six months finally came to a head. Fighting to gain his freedom from his father, moving to a town where he knew no one, being caught in a fire, and now finding out he was kept breathing by a machine for the past three days. Christ, he couldn't even wipe his own eyes with his bandaged hands. It was all too much. Johnny figured he was entitled to a mini meltdown.

Ellen dabbed a soft cloth across Johnny's wet cheeks, and then her gentle hand brushed his curly blond hair back off his face. "It'll be okay, son, you'll see."

"How?" Johnny asked, while he fought to get himself under control. His hands trembled and nausea surged through his weakened body.

"Because you're a strong man and Gabe will accept nothing less than your recovery. He can be very stubborn when he wants something, and you've already fought your way off the ventilator. Johnny, you don't strike me as a man who gives up easily." Ellen continued to stroke his hair, as if calming a frightened child. Johnny realized, in essence, that's what he was to her at that moment. After all, she had already adopted him as her honorary son. "I know it's a lot to take in, but you have Gabe and all of us to rely on now."

He knew Ellen was right. He might have been through hell and still had months of rehab to get through, if not longer, but he now had the one thing he'd never dared dream of before: a family to support and care for him. In the last few years, his father seemed to lose interest in Johnny, and his older brother simply disappeared from his life. After his mother died, he was left with no one he could count on. Johnny sent up a silent plea, hoping and praying that he had finally turned a corner in his life where he was no longer alone.

Chapter Five

Gabe watched as Johnny slept peacefully in their comfortable new orthopaedic king-sized bed that he had delivered late last night before Johnny was released from the hospital—and he did consider it *theirs*. After the last ten days spent with this amazing man, Gabe was positive Johnny was *his*. He could easily admit that Johnny was gorgeous. His curly blond hair and big green eyes were striking, and his taut body might not be as muscular as his own, but Johnny had well-defined muscles that Gabe couldn't wait to explore once Johnny was healed.

Johnny might be small in stature, but his spirit was strong and the stream of visitors he received after only living in town a few months was a testament to the man himself. Janice had cried on Johnny's uninjured shoulder, thanking him for saving her life and keeping his promise to not leave her behind. Her husband was so choked up that he barely spoke and only managed a broken "thank you" while rocking their son Ben in his arms.

Josie had visited each and every day once Johnny was out of danger. The first few times, she had been inconsolable after seeing the extent of Johnny's injuries, especially his abdominal wounds from the glass in the window. Over the following days, and with Johnny's unwavering support, Josie came to terms with the fact that it wasn't her fault that Johnny had been hurt and it was truly an accident. His recovery was finally progressing after the fluid was cleared from his lungs. Gabe didn't like to think about how close he'd come to losing Johnny, and he had to make a conscious effort to not dwell on it. Johnny was safe now in Gabe's home, where he would remain and heal.

Now that they were home, Gabe knew to expect his mother and grandmother at any moment. They probably had old Mrs. Walker reporting from across the street. Food should be arriving shortly thereafter with his three sisters. Then the aunts should be stopping by with their spouses and children. Dad had managed to keep most of the Mason women at bay and away from the hospital, but now all bets were off.

As far as Gabe was aware, only his mom, dad, Sam, and Josie had been to the hospital. After Johnny had taken a turn for the worse, Gabe had lived at the hospital with him, caring for the man he intended to spend a great deal of time with. Thankfully, many of his fellow firefighters were able to pick up Gabe's shifts, allowing him to remain at Johnny's bedside. Brighton was a close-knit community, and Gabe was certainly thankful for that.

"You know I can't sleep if you keep staring at me." Johnny's scratchy voice brought Gabe out of his thoughts.

"Sorry, babe, I'll go out to the kitchen. Do you need anything before I leave?"

"Can I come with you?" Johnny asked softly. Gabe knew his beauty didn't like being alone since the fire, and had awakened numerous times with nightmares.

"Sure, we'll go out to the living room. I'm positive the Mason women will be swooping in at any moment." As if to confirm Gabe's suspicions, the doorbell rang.

Johnny simply laughed at him and shook his head. "See, there's a benefit to my family not speaking to me. You'll never have to worry about the in-laws. Besides, I've met a few of the Masons already, and I haven't run away yet." He stopped to cough. "Not that I could run, but I can shuffle like a pro."

"Their loss is my family's gain. I want you just the way you are, and I'm not letting you go, Johnny. I hope you understand that I'm very serious about us." Gabe brushed a gentle kiss over Johnny's lips, wondering if he would scare Johnny off with that admission. He had been waiting patiently for Johnny to become comfortable enough to express how he felt about Gabe, but so far he had remained quiet.

Before Johnny could respond, the family grew restless and began knocking on the front door. Gabe lifted him, wheezing, into his arms and cradled him close to his chest. Gabe loved his family, but at that moment he honestly considered retracing his steps and hiding out in the bedroom with Johnny for the rest of the day.

*****

Johnny was in way over his head. He'd allowed himself to begin falling in love with this sweet, sexy fireman. He'd never done anything impulsive in his life, but he'd so easily handed his heart and complete and utter trust over to the man carrying him in his arms, toward a family that might not approve of him. True, Johnny had already met Gabe's mom and dad, his cousin Sam, and had actually known Gabe's cousin Josie for months, but this was not a free pass into the graces of the remaining masses of Masons.

Fully expecting Gabe to place him on the couch, Johnny was a bit shocked when Gabe walked straight to the front door while still carrying him. Johnny had to confess he felt safe in Gabe's arms, but as soon as he could perform an activity without gasping for breath or buckling in pain, Johnny swore he'd be on his own two feet again. *The occasional cuddle and carry would surely be okay...* Oh, who the hell was he kidding? Johnny was right where he wanted to be—in Gabe's arms.

Gabe easily shifted Johnny's weight and opened the front door. "Hey, Mom, that was fast. Should we be expecting anyone else?"

"Oh, don't be that way. You knew darn well your father wouldn't be able to hold the rest of the family back once you got your fella home." The small sprite of a woman who had wormed her way into Johnny's heart in a matter of days breezed through the door and straight up to him. "Hello, Johnny, how are you feeling today?"

"Better, Mom," he managed in a scratchy voice.

"You poor dear. Your voice sounds so painful." Ellen placed her tiny hand on Johnny's arm.

"Johnny's not going to be talking very much. He has to let his lungs and throat heal. Doctor's orders, especially since his infection," Gabe commanded as he carefully brushed Johnny's wayward curls from his face yet again. "Also, tell your merry band of women that Johnny needs to rest, so keep the wild plans to a minimum for the time being."

"We promise to not drag him out anywhere until he's healed." Ellen dramatically crossed her heart, but the mischief in her eyes gave Johnny pause. *Wild plans?*

"I'll believe that when I see it." Chief Mason walked in with an elderly lady on his arm. This had to be the notorious Grandmother Rose. "How are you feeling, son?"

"Better, sir," Johnny answered again between gasps.

"Okay, that's it, no more talking. Everybody got that? If not, y'all can leave," Gabe ordered and turned toward the couches. "I'll not have Johnny overdoing it and ending up back in the hospital."

"Understood, son. We'll just have the women do all the talking; should be no problem at all," the chief commented. Grandma Rose promptly smacked him on his huge arm with her tiny manicured hand.

"Don't you be badmouthing the people that control your food, son, unless you're fond of tofu," Grandma Rose spoke while she walked right past Ellen and a contrite chief toward Gabe and Johnny. Gabe leaned forward so that she could kiss both men before sitting down on one of the two oversized couches.

Johnny was positive that, to any average person, these couches would be considered mammoth, similar to most of the furniture in Gabe's house. Johnny was pretty confident that he could get lost on them—seriously, fall asleep and never be found again. After taking a closer look around the room, Johnny realized Gabe's home truly reflected the man. It reminded him of a den designed for warmth and comfort. From the rustic stone fireplace and exposed wooden beams, to the open-concept design covered in natural fabrics and earthy tones, not a hint of color could be seen. Johnny could picture wonderful artwork on the walls and colorful throw pillows. He bet Gabe had no idea what to do with a throw pillow other than to, well, throw it. Yep, he could really add a punch of life to Gabe and their home—Johnny was shocked and quickly reined in his wayward thoughts before they went too far. *This isn't my home.*

Johnny finally noticed that Gabe had stopped walking and was now watching him closely as if trying to read his mind. It was a little unnerving how Gabe could do that.

"You can change anything you like, Johnny, but leave me my chair, okay?" Gabe pointed toward an enormous black leather reclining chair that looked so comfy.

Okay, that could stay.

Johnny simply smiled back at Gabe, both because he was unsure of what to say to such a generous offer and he wasn't supposed to talk. Gabe must have taken that as an agreement and kissed Johnny with as much passion as he dared in front of his family to seal the deal.

"Well, holy cow, Dad was right!" a voice yelled from behind Johnny.

Thankfully, Gabe hugged him a bit closer to his chest, preventing Johnny from jumping straight out of his arms. Instead, it triggered a coughing fit, which prompted women to scatter in search of water and the inhaler that the doctor had sent home with him from the hospital. Gabe sat on the couch with Johnny safely on his lap. His coughing caused tears to run down his face. Vaguely, he was aware of more women entering the house and a few other men. Knowing they must be Gabe's aunts and uncles, Johnny's humiliation was now complete.

"Johnny, look at me. That's it. I need you to take a big breath in."

Johnny nodded, and even though his sight was blurry, he kept his eyes locked on Gabe's, trying to calm himself and breathe in, trusting Gabe to get him through this. Johnny felt his inhaler being pushed to his lips, his bandaged hands stopping him from holding the tube himself. Within moments, he could feel a cooling sensation flowing down his throat and into his burning lungs. Gradually he began to breathe easier.

"There you go, babe. You'll be all right. Just need to keep the excitement down to a dull roar." Gabe brushed his chin over the top of Johnny's head before he kissed his forehead. This seemed to be a more intimate gesture to Johnny than simply kissing him on the lips.

"I'm so sorry, Johnny. I didn't mean to yell like that." Johnny turned to see a distraught young woman standing just a few feet away. He guessed her age to be around twenty. She had dark black hair like Gabe's but bright blue eyes like Ellen's. Easy guess, this had to be a younger sister. "I mean, I was shocked. I've never seen my brother look or act like that. I just...I'm sorry."

She seemed to deflate right in front of him, and Johnny couldn't have this bright young woman sad. "It's okay. I guess I'm still a bit jumpy," Johnny croaked out and gave her what he hoped was a reassuring smile. He truly didn't want her to feel bad.

"Okay, back to the no-talking rule." Johnny nodded his agreement before Gabe went on. "This is my youngest sister,

Francine, but we call her Frannie. She's attending Brighton College, the same as Josie, but Frannie's majoring in English." He could hear the pride in Gabe's voice as he spoke about his sister. No one in Johnny's family had ever spoken of him that way.

"I want to become a teacher someday." The young girl beamed, smiling from ear to ear, and put two bags on the large wooden coffee table in front of Johnny. "I brought lots of stuff for us to do while you're recovering. I know you can't use your hands properly yet, but we'll figure out a way around it."

Frannie's optimism was contagious and Johnny smiled before he snuggled deeper into Gabe's chest and watched Frannie unload board games, a tablet, a chess set, cards, and movies. Grandma Rose, as she asked to be called, sat right up close to Johnny and pulled out photo albums from her oversized bag.

"Now, Johnny," she said. "Before you get all mixed up trying to remember everyone, I'll start at the beginning with pictures."

"Dad, Grandma's brought her photo albums. Can't we just skip over the 'embarrass Gabe' part of the visit?" Gabe groaned into the back of Johnny's head. Johnny turned and gently nuzzled Gabe's cheek to reassure him that all would be fine and that Johnny was actually enjoying himself. He hadn't thought before he acted to soothe Gabe, but the look of complete adoration on Gabe's face was worth anything Johnny could give.

Before Johnny could begin his walk down memory lane with Grandma Rose, the aunts and uncles took the opportunity to introduce themselves one couple at a time. Johnny remembered Josie saying there were lots of first responders in her family, and Johnny quickly realized that was true. There were Cousin Sam's parents Aunt Jane and Uncle Jack, a paramedic; Aunt Dot and Uncle Henry, a psychiatrist; Aunt Casey and her life partner Aunt Marg, a pediatrician; and cousin Josie's parents Aunt Flo and Uncle Jim, a firefighter. Mom explained that the remaining fourteen combined cousins had decided to stay away so as not to completely overwhelm Johnny, but they were guaranteed to come by and introduce themselves throughout the upcoming weeks.

"Johnny, there isn't a way to adequately express how thankful we all are for what you did that day to save our daughter's life." Uncle Jim spoke softly before moving the board games aside and taking a seat on the coffee table in front of Johnny and Gabe, Aunt

Flo at his side. The large man was brought to tears when Josie walked through the front door and came to kneel beside her father. Johnny reached out and placed one bandaged hand on Uncle Jim's leg. He wasn't sure how to comfort the man, so he remained quiet. Gabe wrapped Johnny in the safety of his arms, providing the emotional support Johnny needed.

"When I saw Josie hanging from that window, my heart stopped. I was down on the rig manning the deck gun, knocking down the flames when I saw you throw yourself out of that window, grabbing for my daughter. You're family now, Johnny. Even if you weren't with Gabe, you would be family." Uncle Jim's hands began to shake slightly. "If you ever need anything, anything at all, you let me know. We can never repay you for what you've done, but we'll never forget it either."

The room fell silent and a troop of hummingbirds began manoeuvres in Johnny's stomach. He considered how to respond to Uncle Jim's declaration; the man deserved honesty. "I—I was scared out of my mind. I'm not a hero, sir. If I could've found us any other way out of that building, I would've taken it." *Cough—cough—* "Hell, if I could've left the decisions up to someone else in the room"—*cough*—"I would have, but it just wasn't an option."

"And that's why you're a hero, young man. When it came down to the lives of three women, you stood up. You took control and you saved lives without concern for your own. Whether you want to believe us or not, it won't change how we feel," Uncle Jim explained before he leaned forward and gently hugged Johnny, followed by Aunt Flo and Josie; all were careful of his injuries.

"Whether you believe it or not, babe, you're a hero to this family." Gabe held Johnny snug to his chest. "Now that's definitely enough talking for you. Let's have everyone else take over for now."

Gabe's other two younger sisters, Joanne and Kate, arrived not ten minutes later with their husbands and two children. The little four-year-old boy was Joanne's, and the baby girl was Kate's. Johnny was beginning to get the suspicion that this was a well-timed invasion. Food was cooked, and schedules worked out, so that when Gabe had to work, one of the many family members would be with Johnny.

"You don't have to change your schedules for me." Johnny didn't want everyone to have to put their lives on hold because of him. "I'll heal up and be out of your hair in no time."

A few of the women simply smiled and shook their heads, but Grandma Rose just came right out with what she was thinking. "My grandson won't be wanting to let you go if that constant smile on his face is any indication. So you might as well get used to the family, honey, because you're stuck with us."

Johnny glanced up to Gabe, who looked determined and simply nodded his head in agreement with Grandma Rose's statement. Some women went back to cooking, while others were invading cupboards and closets, calling out items that were needed as Frannie kept a running list. Grandma Rose continued with family photos and hilarious stories. Johnny knew he would love spending time with the women of this family.

He felt a twinge of pain and looked down at his bandaged hands. The doctors couldn't predict how much damage was done to the nerves in his hands or how much mobility he would lose until he was further along in his recovery. Johnny was scared. He had no idea what he would do if he couldn't use his hands. How would he survive or continue in graphic design? He had fought so hard for his career away from his father, and now it could be taken away from him.

"You okay, babe?" Gabe asked. "Are your hands sore?"

Johnny nodded, trying to keep to the no-talking rule as much as possible. He had learned early on that it was useless to play down his injuries and pain; Gabe seemed to know the truth whether Johnny wanted him to or not.

Gabe stood and placed him gently back on the couch. "We'll figure everything out together, Johnny. For now, I'll go get your medication. You just rest." Several Mason men and women watched their interaction with interest and simply smiled or nodded in some sort of silent agreement toward Gabe. At times, it seemed as though the members of the Mason family only had to look at one another to know what the other was thinking without speaking a single word.

"So is telepathy a Mason trait as well, and if so, when do I start my lessons?" Johnny asked the group of men and women gathered on and around the couches. Gabe's laugh was so deep and filled with joy that Johnny couldn't help but smile back at him. When Gabe was happy, he was contagious, and from glancing around the room, Johnny knew his family felt the same way.

"Don't worry, son. You'll catch on soon enough," the chief explained as Gabe carried on into the kitchen to retrieve Johnny's medication and water. He lowered his voice before he continued. "I haven't seen Gabe this happy in a very long time, Johnny. Just keep doing whatever it is you're doing."

Johnny had no idea what he was doing, but he was enjoying spending time with Gabe and his family. They were strong, loving, and hilarious. It hadn't escaped his notice that most of the men in this family were very dominant, take-charge individuals; even the men who married into the family were alpha individuals. But it was obvious the women of the family actually held everything together. The aunts owned a boutique on the main street called Hidden Treasures, selling artwork and crafts from local artists. Both Kate and Joanne were pediatric nurses, and their husbands, Dave and Rick respectively, were both police officers.

Just as Gabe brought back Johnny's medication and a glass of water, a few cell phones and beepers started to go off, including Gabe's.

"Here, sweetheart, take these." Gabe handed Johnny two pills and held the water for him to drink since Johnny couldn't hold a glass yet. Frustrating!

"We have to go, son. Everyone has been called in. We have a retirement home in Jenson on fire, and they're afraid it could spread to the nearby hospital," Chief Mason announced. Johnny noticed a number of the men stood, kissed their family good-bye, and went out the front door. That amazed Johnny, families who spent their whole lives protecting and helping others. Polar opposites of his own family. His father and brother might be doctors, but it wasn't to help others, that was for damn sure.

"Johnny, I've got to go. Mom and Grandma Rose will stay here with you until I come back," Gabe explained as he crouched in front of Johnny and cupped his cheeks with his huge hands.

"So will I," Frannie announced. "I'll help you, Johnny."

Gabe looked upon his youngest sister with such love. "Thank you, Frannie. I'm sure you'll help keep him out of trouble. Now, Johnny, I want you to eat and get some rest. I don't know how long I'll be, but we'll be back as soon as we can."

Johnny didn't like the thought of Gabe going out into danger, but he respected the man's choice to be a firefighter. "Please be safe."

"I will, don't you worry. I have someone important to come home to." Gabe gave him a quick kiss and followed his father out to his truck.

Johnny didn't know what to do. This was the first time since he and Gabe became a couple that Gabe would be going off to fight a fire, and he would have to wait at home and worry.

"He'll be safe, dear," Ellen said softly before adjusting the pillow behind Johnny's head. "I won't lie to you; it doesn't get better with time, and you still worry every time they leave. You have to be sure you love him completely to sign on for this kind of life."

Johnny had to agree. These women lived with men who ran into hell to save people while everyone else was running in the other direction. He respected their strength and courage. Johnny knew he was falling in love with Gabe; he felt it to his very soul. Johnny also knew he would never be able to walk away from the man, but old doubts still lingered. *Why would a man like Gabe want me?*

"I want Gabe in my life any way I can get him." Johnny went with the truth; these women deserved it from him. "I'm falling in love with him."

Ellen's smile lit up her entire face, while his sisters, aunts, and Grandma Rose gathered around to join in the conversation.

"Have you told him, dear?" Ellen asked before she brought the straw up for Johnny to take a much-needed drink of iced tea.

"No. Isn't it too soon? He'll think I'm out of my mind." Johnny thought for sure he was out of his own damn mind, so it wasn't a big jump to think Gabe would be as well. *There was no such thing as love at first sight or even second sight, right?*

"Honey, the way Gabe looks at you now, I'm pretty sure he's already in love with you as well," Aunt Flo announced while the other women simply nodded their agreement.

Johnny had a hard time believing that Gabe felt so strongly about him, but he kept those thoughts to himself. They finished dinner with very little dignity for Johnny as he was forced to allow Ellen to feed him yet again. His hands were so heavily bandaged there was no way he could hold a fork or spoon. The aunts, a few remaining uncles, and the two oldest sisters had left for the evening, and Johnny was just getting settled on the couch to watch a movie with

Frannie, Ellen, and Grandma Rose when the doorbell rang. Ellen went to answer it, and even without a clear view of the front door, no one could miss the tall blond man's entrance.

"Ellen, so good to see you again. Is *my* man home?" The blond literally walked right past a pissed-off-looking Ellen and invited himself straight into the living room.

Who is this guy and who the hell is his "man"?

Frannie stood and cut the man off before he could get any further. "You aren't welcome here, Chris. Gabe made that clear, so take your lying ass back out the way you came."

That was when the rude man finally noticed Johnny bundled on the couch. "Who have we here, the invalid from the hospital? This mouse can't be my replacement. Christ, did he have to stoop that low after I left?" Chris sneered at Johnny. From his designer jeans to his perfect teeth and hair, he was the exact opposite of Johnny.

Johnny had no idea who this person was, but he had some sort of relationship with Gabe and hated the fact that Johnny was in this house. That much was clear. He could feel his chest tighten, a sure sign of the onset of a coughing fit, and Johnny desperately didn't want whoever this Chris was to see him coughing his lungs out.

"You need to leave, now." Johnny croaked out, feeling the rattle starting deep in his chest. *Shoot, no talking, stop talking.* The women looked approvingly at him. Even though he was injured, he wasn't going to sit back and have someone push him around. Not anymore.

"What the hell is wrong with you? Tell me *my* Gabe didn't just pick up some stray he felt sorry for?" The disdain dripping from Chris's every word and his curled lip and cold eyes were truly amazing to Johnny. He thought his father was the only man who could pull off such contempt.

"That's it! Get out of this house right now or I'll drag your worthless ass out." Frannie was fuming, and Johnny noticed Mom was now on the phone. Grandma Rose stood right in front of him as if guarding Johnny. God, he loved these women.

Johnny could hear sirens in the distance and he figured Mom had called in the cavalry. He would have laughed, but he was beginning to gasp again. Johnny knew he soon would be coughing. He needed to calm down. Unfortunately, Chris didn't want calm; he wanted batshit crazy, and he actually lunged at Johnny. He would have knocked him and Grandma Rose off the couch if Frannie hadn't tackled the asshole to the ground. Apparently, Frannie knew self-defense. *Go girl!*

Uniformed officers came running into the house just as Frannie pinned Chris to the floor. The police officers handcuffed the now irate man and dragged him out of the house. "He's mine, you worthless little shit. He wants to marry me!"

That was news and the last straw for his attempted calm. Johnny couldn't catch his breath and began coughing violently. Through blurry eyes, he watched Mom run in with his inhaler.

"Johnny, honey, you look at me. I need you to calm and take a breath in." Grandma Rose looked him straight in the eyes. "You will not allow that awful man to hurt you and Gabe. You're stronger than that. Now breathe in."

Johnny obediently sucked in a bit of air and felt the mist working its way down his throat and into his burning, painful lungs. After a few minutes, it became a bit easier to breathe and Johnny was able to sit up slightly with Frannie's help. He looked around the living room to find an EMT and Joanne's husband, Rick, in his police uniform standing nearby. Groaning from embarrassment, Johnny lay back down on the couch, hoping the damn thing would actually swallow him up. No such luck. The EMT crouched beside the couch and gave him a friendly smile.

"Hi, Johnny, I'm Royce. You might not remember me, but I work with Gabe. I think it's best if we take you back to the hospital and have you checked out." Royce leaned over and wrapped a blood pressure cup around Johnny's upper arm.

"I'm fine, but thank"—*cough*—"you for your help." Johnny was not in any way wanting to go back to the hospital.

"Here, Johnny." Mom leaned over and placed her cell phone to Johnny's ear.

Confused, Johnny leaned into the phone and croaked, "Hello?"

"Johnny, don't speak." Gabe's voice was intermixed with sirens in the background. "You'll go to the hospital with Royce. It's not open for discussion. I'll be with you as soon as I can."

Now, what happened next Johnny would blame on the shock of the events over the last couple days, his questionable sanity, or a full moon, if there even was one. "Fine. Love you too," he croaked and carefully pushed the off button with his nose before Gabe could respond.

Shooting Mom a pleading look before lying back down on the couch, Johnny was dreading going to the hospital. "Don't give me that look, young man. I've dealt with men bigger than you my entire life. Besides, I didn't call him. His father received a report that police and EMS were called out here. Gabe was a little concerned, to put it mildly, and if my son got you to go to the hospital, then so be it. Now, let's move out!"

"Yes, ma'am," Johnny and Royce said in unison before Royce and his teammate lifted him onto the gurney and they were off back to the same place he had just left that morning. Johnny was devastated.

Chapter Six

Gabe was furious. How dare Chris come into his house and try to attack his Johnny. Shit, and on the first day he had Johnny home. *How was that even possible? Is Chris watching my house?*

Gabe had spent the next four hours fighting to keep the fire contained to the retirement residence and trying to calm his racing heart. Johnny had said he loved him; well, he actually said he loved him *too*, which meant Johnny knew how Gabe felt about him and he felt the same for Gabe. He just prayed that Chris hadn't screwed this up royally for him. Gabe finally found a man who filled the empty places in his heart, and he wasn't letting him go. For years he had been living half a life. Sure, he had his family, friends, and work that he loved, but he was alone and afraid to trust again. Now he knew with absolute certainty that Johnny was the perfect man for him, and it filled Gabe with a profound feeling of contentment and peace.

When he arrived back at the firehouse, Royce was waiting for him. "Gabe, you look about ready to kill someone. You need to calm down before you go to Johnny. The guy's been through enough."

Gabe stopped in his tracks and lowered his head in disgust. He knew Royce was right. He was ready to kill anyone who dared to hurt Johnny, and he needed to get a grip on his anger. "You're right. I just…Royce, I finally—"

"It's okay, buddy. Hell, if I had someone…" Royce looked off for a moment, and Gabe immediately felt his heart plummet. Royce's husband had died tragically in a car accident over three years earlier, and Royce had never been the same. His friends had hoped that with time Royce would heal, but the life and joy had been sucked right out of him, and it seemed as though he might never fully recover.

Gabe reached out to Royce and gave his friend a hug. Neither of them spoke for several moments, allowing Royce the time he needed to snap out of his thoughts. "You better get going. I know it has to be hell what you're going through with Chris showing up like that and Johnny back in the hospital. You need anything, you call me anytime."

"Thank you." There was nothing more to say. These men were part of his extended family and understood how important Johnny was to him and the hell he went through when Chris took off. Gabe had been there for Royce, just as every other person in this department had been, and they would all be there for Gabe—there was never a doubt.

He knew Johnny was safe at the hospital, but it still seemed to take forever to stow all the gear, shower, and have the chief drive him there since his truck was still at his house. Before his dad's truck was even in park, Gabe was out the passenger door and striding into the emergency department. There were familiar faces everywhere, but not the one he was desperate to find.

His cousin Sam stood behind the nurses' station and raised his hands in surrender when Gabe walked up. "He's okay, Gabe. Come on, I'll take you to his room."

Gabe was beginning to wonder exactly what he looked like to make Sam so compliant because even on a good day, his flamboyant cousin was about as compliant as a rattlesnake.

Raising one eyebrow in question, Sam smiled and answered, "You look about ready to blow, cuz."

"Sorry, Sam. It's been a long day." Gabe hung his head and apologized.

"Don't worry about it; you have a right. Who would have thought that asshole would just randomly show up and attack Johnny, especially after you had him kicked out of the hospital?" Sam sighed as he came around the huge glassed-in desk and led Gabe and the chief toward the elevators. "Johnny is nothing like Chris, thank God! I would have to slap you silly if you hooked up with anyone like that jerk ever again."

"Can't disagree with you on that one." Gabe laughed for the first time since leaving Johnny earlier.

"Hey, the guy saved you from the aunts." Sam shook his head before getting on the elevator and pushing the button for the third floor. "He's golden in my books."

"Well, I'm glad they finally dropped the charges against you, Sam." Gabe smiled innocently, desperate to keep a straight face. His dad, on the other hand wasn't as in control, which was apparent by the laughter coming from the corner.

"Laugh all you want, you two, but being arrested by Marshals while on a blind date your loving aunts set up *is not funny!*"

"Oh come on, how was Aunt Dot supposed to know there was a warrant out for the guy's arrest?" Now Gabe was laughing just as loudly as his dad.

"It wasn't a warrant; it was a man hunt!" Sam hollered just before he broke out laughing himself. Though it wasn't funny at the time, Sam had been cleared of any involvement in his date's thieving escapades. At the very least, it gave Sam an automatic lifetime ban on the aunts' matchmaking attempts.

Sam led them to a darkened room. It was almost 2:00 a.m. "They moved him up here about three hours ago. They want to keep him in for another few days, Gabe."

Gabe froze. "Why do they want to keep him? What's wrong with Johnny?" All kinds of scenarios were running through his head. What if Johnny had been hurt worse than he was told? What if the damage to his lungs was worse or if he had developed another infection?

"Doctor Green is trying him on a different medication to help heal his lungs with less pain to Johnny. But he has to be connected to oxygen and monitored during treatment, so it's best he stays here. The doctor asked to be paged when you arrived so that he could explain everything to you himself, but he was needed in surgery, so he'll be a couple hours at least," Sam explained as if it was completely normal. Gabe knew he was overreacting, but hell, this was *his* Johnny.

"Son, why don't you go on in and send your mother out. I'll bring your truck in the morning. I don't imagine you're leaving here tonight."

"As long as Johnny's here, I'll be here. Thanks for everything, Sam, Dad." Gabe hugged them both and turned toward Johnny's room.

"You have to tell him, son." His dad spoke softly but the words held enough pain to stop Gabe in his tracks.

"I didn't think we would have to cross this bridge so soon," Gabe admitted, feeling the sharp edge of a long-ago pain cutting through his well-healed wounds. All he wanted to do was start a life with Johnny, and now his past was bearing down on him.

"He's a good man. A good match for you, son, and he loves you. That's obvious, but don't let Chris destroy it before you even get a chance to start."

"Listen to your father," Ellen said as she softly closed the door to Johnny's room and joined the men in the hallway. "He needs to know. Chris said some pretty vulgar and condescending things, and Johnny needs an explanation."

Gabe clenched his jaw and actually felt himself getting hotter, causing his palms to sweat. The need to track down Chris and run him out of town was overpowering.

"Go in there. Johnny needs you, and you need him. Just be honest; he'll understand." Ellen kissed Gabe on the cheek, took his dad's hand, and walked back down the hall toward the elevators.

Gabe had to take a few moments to calm himself down and think before he went into Johnny's room. He had no idea how he was going to explain being with a man he believed loved him only to find out how big a sucker he really was. Years of plans—plans of marriage and plans for children—all gone because Gabe was just another easy mark. It didn't matter how many times his friends and family told Gabe it wasn't his fault. In the end, it was.

*****

Johnny heard whispers of a conversation outside his room but couldn't quite make out what was being said. He had been asleep for almost two hours and only woke as Mom left his room. For what felt like the hundredth time, Johnny tugged on the mask covering his nose and mouth. He felt suffocated but he'd been warned numerous times not to remove it.

In truth, Johnny knew why he was so unsettled—Gabe wasn't here with him. Mom had told Johnny that the fire crews had put out the blaze and stopped the fire from spreading to the hospital and everyone was safe, but that had been hours ago and still no Gabe.

Johnny wondered if perhaps this Chris meant more to Gabe than even his family knew. Maybe he decided Johnny was too big a pain to be bothered? Truthfully, Chris was handsome, tall, strong, polished—in fact, he was everything Johnny wasn't. How could he even compete? Maybe he should just bow out gracefully before he embarrassed himself any further.

The creak of the door alerted Johnny that he wasn't alone. He turned to see the man that he loved and, he just realized, couldn't keep. *This sucked.*

"Hey, babe, you're awake. I thought you'd be sleeping." Gabe came to his bedside immediately and kissed Johnny's forehead, avoiding the dreaded mask still covering most of his face, or at least that was what Johnny hoped. "I don't want you to talk, Johnny. You need to rest your lungs."

Johnny was perfectly fine with not talking. He had absolutely no idea what to say anyway. *Sorry I ruined your reunion with your fiancé?* Not likely. Gabe looked upset; maybe he felt bad for having to send him on his way while injured. But Johnny had thought ahead and had the nurse bring in information on home care. That way, Gabe wouldn't have to feel bad about sending him home. He could hire a health care worker to come in daily. It would kill him, but he would do it for the man he loved. Gabe turned to place his bag on the floor by the bedside table and picked up the booklet on home care.

"What's this, Johnny?" Gabe's voice hardened as he asked, but before Johnny could even open his mouth to answer, Gabe stopped him. "Wait, you're not supposed to be talking, so I'll do the talking and you do the listening, okay?"

Johnny simply nodded, a bit confused by Gabe's angry reaction to the home care booklet. Honestly, he thought Gabe would be relieved. Gabe carried a chair closer to Johnny's bed and sat down heavily. It seemed as if Gabe didn't have the strength to stand any longer; he buried his head in his hands. Johnny couldn't help himself, and reached out to brush his bandaged hand over Gabe's short, dark hair—needing any sort of physical contact.

Gabe didn't even raise his head as he spoke. "You deserve to know who that person was that attacked you today."

Gabe finally looked up. The pain in his dark eyes hit Johnny hard and caused his heart to beat a tiny bit faster. "I'm so sorry that Chris tried to assault you. He should have never been anywhere near you, and if I have anything to say about it, he'll never be again." Gabe reached up and ran his hand down Johnny's arm; it felt like a caress. Totally confused at the direction this conversation was taking, Johnny remained silent for a moment because this was the strangest "it's not you, it's me" speech he'd ever received.

Gabe seemed to be caught in some internal struggle, and Johnny couldn't let this carry on. The poor guy had been nothing but wonderful to him. It wasn't Gabe's fault that Johnny had fallen in love with him. Gabe didn't deserve to have to feel sorry for loving someone else, even if it was that asshole Chris.

"It's okay, Gabe. I can make arrangements for home care. You don't have to worry about me. I won't press charges against your fiancé."

There, that sounded confident and not like my heart was breaking.

Gabe stood up so fast his chair crashed to the floor, and before Johnny could even register what was happening, Gabe had him cradled in his arms lying on the bed. Amazingly, his mask had stayed on.

"I know we've just started out, but I can't lose you." Gabe pressed his forehead to Johnny's. He could feel a tremble run through Gabe's body. "He isn't my fiancé. At one time, I thought we would be married and, hopefully, have children, but I was sucked right into his lies. We were together just over a year. He moved into my home, and we were making plans for the future. Chris played his part well. Friends and family began to make comments about Chris's odd behaviour and seeing him around town at strange times of day when he told me he was at work. But did I listen? Of course not, because the Chris that was home with me wasn't the same Chris he showed everyone else."

The self-loathing and pain in Gabe's voice broke something deep inside Johnny and he couldn't hold back the tears for this poor man. Gabe held him closer but averted his eyes before he continued. "People I've known my entire life, people that I trust with my life, and I didn't believe them. I gave Chris more trust than I did my own family."

Johnny had no idea when he had begun stroking Gabe's chest to comfort him, but he needed the contact even if it was through layers of gauze, and he thought Gabe might need it as well.

"I turned my back on my family and friends when I chose not to listen to them. This was all my fault. I believed his lies and when he took off one day without a word, I'm sure I was the only one surprised. He'd cleaned out the house of anything of value he could sell and emptied the joint bank account. Thank God I never gave him the combination to my safe or access to my personal accounts. Anything of real importance to me was in the safe and the bulk of my money he couldn't touch. Maybe deep down I knew not to give him access to those things."

Johnny tried to speak, to comfort him, but Gabe stopped him with just one devastated look. "Babe, please let me get the rest out. It gets worse."

Worse?

"At the end, before he took off, we had been organizing our wedding and even had lined up a gestational surrogate for our supposed children. I was a fucking idiot to trust him. The woman from the agency Chris had interviewed and 'thoroughly background checked' was actually his sister. She wasn't a real surrogate and had tried to get a portion of the fee up front before even going to the fertility clinic. I became suspicious and refused to even consider her before speaking to the agency. She disappeared about the same time as Chris. I haven't seen or heard from him in years, since the day he left right up until a few months ago. He sent me e-mails, which I deleted unopened, and then he showed up at the hospital when you were unconscious." Gabe gently cupped the side of his face, making sure he made eye contact with Johnny before continuing. "He never made it anywhere near you, baby. I had him out of your room and out of the hospital almost immediately."

Holy shit, that asshole! Taking advantage of Gabe's dream of having a family. Who does that?

"That was over two years ago, and you're the first man I've trusted since, outside my family and friends. The odd thing about that whole situation was that I had never given up that much control ever in my life, and, Johnny, I'm sorry but it'll be even harder for me to give up control now. That's something you need to know right from the start."

Johnny gave a soft laugh then gasped for air before saying, "I already know that. I trust you, Gabe. I know you were there keeping me safe. You'll always keep me safe." He knew down to his soul that Gabe would never do anything to harm him and would only look out for his best interests. He wasn't naïve enough to think there weren't going to be a few disagreements in their future, but they would work it out; they just needed to be willing to try.

Johnny had always considered himself to be a smart man, and he'd be damned if he was going to throw away the best thing to happen to him just because some jerk showed up. The only way he was leaving was if Gabe asked him to, and even then Johnny would be hard-pressed to listen.

Gabe's dark eyes cleared from his sad thoughts and past pain. He gently ran his thumb along Johnny's jaw and up into his hair, and damn if that didn't just make certain parts of Johnny perk right up. *I'm hurt, not dead.*

"You'll stay with me?" Gabe said softly. Johnny wasn't sure if that was a question or statement, but he nodded in agreement just in case. He wanted no misunderstandings. "I love you, Johnny."

"I love you too, Gabe." Gabe gently removed Johnny's oxygen mask before giving him a kiss filled with love and the promise of future passion. Johnny would have never thought that it was possible to feel clear emotions in a kiss, but Gabe made him a believer. He could feel Gabe's love for him loud and clear. He wouldn't doubt what Gabe felt for him again. He was a very lucky man and knew it.

Saying yes and staying with the man he loved was that simple and that complicated all at once. There was nothing more that needed to be said; they loved each other. Johnny knew the facts, made his choice, and his choice was Gabe.

Chapter Seven

Two weeks later

The interior of Hidden Treasures felt more like your favorite aunt's house than a store. Well, in Johnny's case, the store was owned by Gabe's four aunts and his mom, so it wasn't too far off base. The store smelled like fresh cinnamon rolls, which Aunt Flo baked religiously every morning while the others dusted and arranged beautiful displays of stained glass, jewelry, carvings, metal sculptures, colorful artwork, and much more from local artists. Several carved wood pieces of local wildlife and paintings of a nearby lake now graced Gabe's house.

Though several of Johnny's belongings had made their way over to Gabe's house, he still felt like a guest. No matter what Gabe said or the fact that they slept together in the master bedroom every night—though without sex until Johnny was physically cleared—it didn't help ease his worry that once he was better he would have to leave. He wasn't sure what it would take to make Gabe's house feel like home. In fact, if Johnny were honest with himself, he hadn't felt as if he had a real home since his mother had died. Perhaps he never would.

"Do you want to walk over to the diner with me and pick up lunch, Johnny?" Aunt Jane asked as she walked out of the back storage room carrying a stunning new watercolor painting delivered that morning.

Johnny's lungs had been healing very quickly after his second visit to the hospital, and all his stitches had been removed, but his hands were still mainly wrapped, making it difficult for him to handle daily tasks. Gabe was on shift at the fire station and refused to leave Johnny on his own just yet, so here he sat behind the counter as Aunt Jane and Aunt Flo helped customers and unloaded stock. Johnny desperately needed to feel useful again.

"How about I walk down to the diner and pick up our order and bring it back here for lunch?" Johnny suggested, liking the idea more and more. He could use the small walk across town to clear his mind. "It shouldn't take me too long."

"Are you sure, Johnny? How's your breathing today?" Aunt Jane asked, clearly not liking the idea of letting him go out on his own.

"Oh, let the poor boy go. He has to be suffocating under everyone's care. Johnny's well enough to walk down to the diner on his own." Aunt Flo winked at Johnny to let him know he had one sister on his side.

"But what about his hands? How can he carry the bag without hurting his hands?" Aunt Jane wasn't ready to give up just yet, but Johnny wasn't either.

"Just loan me one of your fabric reusable bags with the handles. Jesse can put our lunches in the bag and I can put it over my good arm." There, that sounded logical to Johnny, and before Aunt Jane could come up with anything else, he slipped the handle of the bag over his arm and headed for the front door. "I'll be back in less than ten minutes."

The tiny bell tinkling over the door as Johnny left the shop proclaimed his freedom. Okay, Johnny knew he was being a little dramatic and it wasn't all that bad, but he still took the time to enjoy the sun high in the sky on this cloudless summer day.

The air was thick with the smell of roses coming from the garden surrounding the library across the street. The sweet smell reminded him of the oasis Gabe had made for him inside his greenhouse. Once Mom mentioned the joy Johnny displayed in the hospital after being given the orchids both times, Gabe had immediately gone out and bought a large, comfortable reclining chair. He'd placed it in the greenhouse, filled it with pillows, and proclaimed it to be Johnny's spot. Now, in truth, that was where Johnny could be found most days, reading and relaxing, when home. He loved Gabe so completely. To anyone else the gift wouldn't have meant much, but to him it was the world.

Several people called out in greeting from across the street, waving as they walked by. In the past few weeks, Johnny had met more people than he could possibly keep straight, but it felt amazing to be part of a community. For the first time in his life, Johnny felt accepted just the way he was. No one wanted to change him or cared what his last name was. It was amazing and scary all at the same time because Johnny had learned painfully that peace never lasted long. He had felt it on one occasion while away at college, but it was fleeting once his father arrived. After that one unwelcomed visit, regular reports were sent to his father from each of Johnny's professors and his roommate suddenly found other accommodations, leaving Johnny alone once again.

Five minutes into his walk, the small hairs on the back of Johnny's neck stood on end. He looked around, but nothing seemed out of place. Johnny couldn't shake the feeling of being watched and quickened his pace toward the diner. The sunny streets suddenly felt like they were getting darker and closing in on him, but nothing stood out. He felt foolish by the time he walked through the diner doors. Johnny had been working hard to regain his self-confidence since leaving his father's estate, only to find himself almost running into the diner because he was spooked. *I guess twenty-nine years of fear and self-loathing will take more time to reprogram than I thought.* Several more people shouted out hellos as Johnny forced a smile and joined Jesse at the counter.

Jesse was new to town. According to the White Hair Crew, he had drifted into town looking for a new start. He looked to be only about twenty-five, but his weary brown eyes told Johnny he'd seen too much in that short time. Grandma Rose took a liking to him right off, which was a stamp of approval if there ever was one, and Jesse found himself with a job as a part-time cook and full-time waiter at the diner. He also was able to rent a room in the small apartment above it and began his new life all within the first week; the "Crew" worked fast.

"Hey, Johnny, it's good to see you out on your own," Jesse joked. He knew how much Johnny had been chomping at the bit to feel normal again. Although now, with his tiny hairs screaming out warnings, he wondered if it would be odd to ask Jesse to walk him back. "You here to pick up your aunts' order?"

"Yes, thanks, Jesse." He handed the bag over to Jesse who filled it with takeout containers. Johnny couldn't help looking over his shoulder and out the front window, but no one was there. He felt like he was losing his damn mind.

"Are you okay, Johnny?" Jesse asked, still holding the bag in his hand without handing it over to Johnny.

"Yeah, I think I just freaked myself out is all. It's nothing." Johnny felt stupid now that he thought about it.

"How about you let me decide if it's nothing." Jesse's voice was tinged with concern. He stood only a few feet away, still not releasing the bag to Johnny and not looking like he was going to without an explanation.

"Well, when I was walking over here, the hairs on the back of my neck stood up and it felt like I was being watched." Johnny rubbed his bandaged hand over his neck, trying to ease the feeling. "But no one's there. It's in my head; I'm just working myself up."

Jesse looked out the diner window and scanned the area before yelling into the back kitchen. "Clem, I'm walking Johnny over to his aunts' shop. I'll be back in a few minutes."

Clem, a giant of a man, came to the front, wiping his big hands on a dishcloth hanging from his apron. Johnny absently wondered if there was something in the water around here making most of the men the size of bears. "No problem, Jesse. Wanna stop and get the mail at the post office while you're out?"

"Sure, boss man." Jesse smiled at Clem. "There isn't another one of those packages in there for a special someone? Oh, I don't know, maybe a certain librarian…?"

"Go, you troublemaker, and leave my packages out of this," Clem grumbled happily.

"I'm just saying, if you gave Rick the chance, I'm sure he would be more than happy to check out your package." Jesse laughed, dodging the dishcloth thrown at his head. "We're going, boss man…so testy."

Jesse led Johnny out of the diner and scanned the area again.

"It's okay, Jesse. I just got myself all worked up over nothing."

"Well, it's better to be safe. If you felt it, I believe it. You can't go around ignoring things like that, Johnny. Trusting my gut has saved my ass a few times," Jesse assured him. Johnny had a feeling he spoke from experience and not just in an attempt to make Johnny feel less embarrassed.

Jesse kept a look out while telling Johnny all about Clem's crush on Rick, the librarian, and vice versa. They were exact opposites, and if Jesse could be believed both were trying desperately not to let the other know how they felt.

"It's a damn soap opera, Johnny. I swear I'm going to have to come up with a way to get them together before they miss out on something amazing. Chances like that don't come around every day." Jesse swore before getting a faraway look on his face.

"You're really a softy, aren't you, Jesse? You have all these tattoos and ride a badass motorcycle, but you have a heart the size of Texas. I can tell; no use in denying it. Besides, Grandma Rose already spoke highly of you, so you're as good as in around here." Johnny laughed at the stunned expression on Jesse's face, as if being accepted hadn't even crossed his mind as possible.

"Well, just don't go telling too many folks or my cover will be blown," Jesse teased before walking across the crosswalk a block down from Hidden Treasures. "I really like this town. It has a feel to it, you know?"

The sudden squeal of tires was the only thing that alerted them to a silver car speeding toward them out of a side street.

"Look out, Johnny!" Jesse yelled before he pushed Johnny out of the way, unavoidably placing himself in front of the vehicle. Jesse's right leg was struck by the car's passenger-side fender, and the blow threw him a few feet away from Johnny.

The car continued to race down the street and around the corner, vanishing and assuring Johnny that he could crawl to Jesse's side. People were screaming for help and running in his direction. The aunts came sprinting out of their shop.

"Jesse, can you hear me?" Johnny grabbed Jesse's limp hand, praying to God that the man who had just saved his life wouldn't lose his own. "Jesse, can you open your eyes? Please open your eyes!"

"Johnny, an ambulance is on the way. What happened?" Aunt Jane asked, while applying pressure to a wound on Jesse's leg that Johnny hadn't seen in his panic.

"A car came out of nowhere. Jesse pushed me out of the way—he saved my life, Aunt Jane. He can't die!" Johnny screamed, terrified Jesse would indeed die.

Jesse moaned before he opened his eyes. "I'm not going anywhere. At least, not yet."

"The ambulance is on its way, young man. You just lie back," Aunt Flo said softly. "Johnny's Uncle Jack is working today and on his way. They'll take good care of you, I promise."

"Th-thank you, ma'am," Jesse said between clenched teeth. The pain he was in was obvious. "Can someone call Clem and tell him I—I can't make it back today p-please?"

"I'm right here, son. Don't you be worrying about nothing right now." Clem leaned over and placed a few clean towels under Jesse's head. Police had arrived and were moving the crowd back. Kate's husband, Dave, was talking quietly to Aunt Flo.

"You just hold on, okay? My family will be here soon to help you." Johnny held Jesse's hand as best he could with his own still bandaged, but he'd be damned if he would let go of the man who saved his life, no matter how painful it was.

The sounds of sirens pierced through the crowd as an ambulance and fire truck pulled up. Chief Mason, Gabe, Uncle Jim, Lee, and Ben raced over with their bags and a backboard from the fire truck. EMTs Uncle Jack and Royce wheeled a stretcher from the back of their rig through the crowd and began to work on stabilizing Jesse. Royce carefully brushed his hand along Jesse's jaw and whispered something into his ear, causing Jesse to smile. Johnny was gently moved aside and found himself in Gabe's strong arms. *Safe.*

"Jesse pushed me out of the way. That car would have hit me, Gabe. It was coming straight at me." The severity of the situation was finally hitting home for Johnny. Someone had tried to run him down and poor Jesse was the one hurt. Johnny began to shake uncontrollably in Gabe's arms. He was quickly carried back into the shop and away from the crowds.

"Easy, baby, I've got you. You're safe now." Gabe murmured the reassuring words into Johnny's ear over and over again while rocking him from side to side.

Eventually Johnny was calm enough to breathe normally again. He hadn't even noticed he was hyperventilating or that Gabe had Johnny's inhaler in his hand. They watched as the ambulance sped away and the family walked back into the shop.

"We have to go to the hospital, Gabe. Jesse doesn't have anyone," Johnny pleaded, knowing how scary it could be finding yourself in the hospital all alone.

"We will, sweetheart, but I need you to tell us what happened first if you can." Gabe was assuring as he continued to hold Johnny safely in his arms, seemingly in no hurry to release him, for which Johnny was very grateful.

Dave took out his notepad along with another officer. Dad and the rest of the family who were on scene stood to the side. "Did you see who was driving the car, Johnny?"

"No. It was silver and came at us so fast. Jesse yelled at me to get out of the way, and then he pushed me just before the car hit him. The car would have hit me, Dave. I have no doubt about that, but I didn't look up to see who was driving. Maybe Jesse did. We have to go now, Gabe, please."

"Of course, Johnny. I'll take you there right now." Gabe set him on his feet and dug through his pockets. "Aunt Flo, can I take your truck? I'll leave the keys for mine. It's at the station."

"Of course, you go right ahead, Gabe. Jim will bring me your truck after his shift. Then we'll all meet you at the hospital." Aunt Flo and Gabe exchanged keys.

"But you're working, Gabe," Johnny began to argue. He'd caused Gabe to miss enough time from work already and wasn't going to add to it.

"I can't go back to work now, Johnny. Not with someone out there trying to run you down," Gabe stated as he gently held Johnny's face between his hands before kissing him fiercely, unconcerned of who stood around. Johnny felt Gabe's love along with his trembles of fear and understood that they both needed this connection to reassure themselves that they were both alive and safe.

"Gabe's right, Johnny. It's best if he stays with you now. I'll call a few more men in, just in case anything else comes up," Gabe's dad assured him, and placed his big hand on Johnny's shoulder. "Jesse has the Mason family to take care of him now."

"Thank you, Dad," Johnny answered softly, trying desperately to hold it together.

"Johnny, why was Jesse walking you back to the shop? Was there a problem at the diner?" Dave asked. The tight lines around his mouth and eyes, along with the barely suppressed growl in his voice were unmistakeable, but thankfully that anger was directed at whoever was behind the wheel and not Johnny.

"When I was walking to the diner I got a strange feeling that someone was watching me, but I didn't see anyone or anything out of the ordinary. I told Jesse and he said to trust my feelings and that he would walk me back to the shop. If he hadn't, I would've..." Johnny's voice finally cracked and a sob broke free.

"Shhh, it's okay, sweetheart. You're safe." Gabe hugged Johnny close to his chest, seemingly unwilling to let him get even a foot away from him.

"But who would want to hurt me? I don't know a lot of people and everyone in town has been so kind to me. There was only one— *shit.*" Johnny managed to stop himself before he said Chris's name. No one had heard from Chris once he'd been released from jail. Gabe had him charged with trespassing and left it at that, hoping it was a strong enough message to never come back. "But it couldn't be, could it?"

Gabe looked like he was deep in thought before he wrapped his arm even tighter around Johnny and led him toward the door. "We can't count Chris out. No one has seen him, but that doesn't mean he isn't still around. I just can't figure out why he ever dared to come back here."

"We'll meet you at the hospital, Gabe. I need to speak to Jesse as soon as he's stable just in case he was able to see the driver," Dave said before leaving for his squad car.

The chief drove the fire truck back to the station with the rest of their crew, instructing Gabe to call him with any news. Mom met them in the hospital waiting room. Jesse was already in surgery to repair a fractured tibia and shattered kneecap. The surgery involved metal rods, wire, pins, and screws; Johnny began to gag and ran for the washroom after hearing what Jesse had to go through. *This is all my fault.*

Royce had been sitting with them since Mom, Gabe, and Johnny arrived and hadn't moved except to go get updates from the desk. Johnny knew Royce was a good friend of Gabe's and had lost his husband years earlier in a car accident, but he had no idea he was Jesse's friend as well. When he'd asked Royce how the two had met, the answer shocked Johnny but seemed to make complete sense to Gabe.

"Today—I met him for the first time today. At breakfast before my shift." Royce spoke as if stunned by what he himself was admitting. A warm smile replaced his worry for a brief moment. "I went into the diner and there he was, and now I just can't bring myself to leave him."

"That's the exact same feeling I had when I first met my Johnny. That's all it took," Gabe admitted and tightened his hold around Johnny. "I thank God every day that I found him." Johnny felt the love and warmth spread through his cold, tired body. He thanked God every day for Gabe as well.

Royce remained quiet after that; he seemed deep in thought. Johnny couldn't help but wonder if he was thinking of his deceased husband. They had been high school sweethearts, together over ten years. Gabe had explained to Johnny how devastated Royce had been and that he hadn't dated a soul in over three years. But here Royce was, waiting for word on a man he had only just met that morning but was unable to leave. Johnny hoped that both men would find the love he and Gabe were lucky enough to have found.

Over the next few hours, more and more family and friends began to stream into the waiting room. It had been over six hours since they'd begun Jesse's surgery and still no word. Dave came into the room with a file in his hands. He looked at Dad before coming to sit in front of Johnny, who had a feeling he wasn't going to like this.

"Johnny, Gabe, officers had a chance to speak with Jesse for a few moments before he was taken into surgery and, thankfully, he was able to identify the driver of the car. He gave us a description and we were able to show him ten different mug shots. Jesse immediately picked out this one." With that said, Dave opened the file and turned it so that Johnny could see the red, sweaty face staring back at him. Chris.

"Chris is trying to kill me?" Johnny couldn't even comprehend what Dave had just told them. He just stared blankly at the photo of a man he didn't even really know, who apparently tried to run him down. A cold chill ran down Johnny's spine and he began to shake. Gabe immediately gathered him into his arms, and Johnny buried his face into the side of Gabe's neck, trying to calm himself. Gabe stroked his back, speaking softly into Johnny's ear, telling him he would protect him and how much he loved him.

Of course the doctor would choose that exact moment to walk into the waiting room.

"Jesse Tribalt's family?"

Johnny stood along with Royce and every other Mason in the room. The doctor simply shook his head and spoke to everyone. "Jesse made it through surgery just fine. We were able to get the most serious of his injuries stabilized, but there'll be months of physical therapy ahead of him. We'll deal with that later. Right now we just need to make sure he heals properly without complications. Now only two of you at a time can see him until he's moved to his own room."

"Johnny, why don't you and Royce go and see Jesse. We'll wait for you here," Gabe suggested before kissing the top of Johnny's head. Johnny knew the family would want to huddle anyway with the news that Chris was out there somewhere, apparently planning Johnny's demise....

Okay, a bit too dramatic even for me.

Johnny just didn't want to deal with anything more from Chris tonight. He would deal with that asshole tomorrow. "Yes, I think that's best." Johnny didn't mean for his anger at the situation to come out now, but it was so close to the surface that the best course of action was to simply follow the doctor and Royce out of the room, and to face Jesse. The poor man had taken the pain aimed at him and saved his life. Johnny knew this was all his fault. How would Jesse ever forgive him?

*****

Gabe knew this was all his fault. How the hell would Johnny, let alone Jesse, ever forgive him? He stared at the door long after Johnny had left, fighting his need to follow his lover.

"He will, Gabe. Johnny may be understandably upset right now, but he doesn't blame you for any of this." Grandma Rose took Gabe's arm and led him to a seat. Gabe hadn't spoken out loud; perhaps this "family telepathy" thing of Johnny's might have some merit. "And Jesse's never struck me as someone who laid blame at the wrong feet. What we need to be concentrating on now is finding Chris and taking care of and protecting both injured men."

Grandma Rose was never one to sit idly by when things needed to be done. Gabe straightened and squared his shoulders. He knew he couldn't let Chris destroy the future he had planned with the man he loved. "You're right. We have plans to make. We have to find

Chris before he has a chance to hurt anyone else. I just don't understand what he wants. He honestly believes I would take him back. That's insane."

Dave opened the file again and pulled out a few more pieces of paper. "After we arrested Chris and took him from your house, I had a feeling something wasn't quite right. Chris was acting violent one moment and calm the next. He was sweating even with the air conditioning on, and then he seemed almost confused at one point. I didn't find anything on him other than his wallet and keys, so I brought Doc Green over to have a look at him. Doc suspected some sort of drug use and decided to run some bloodwork on him, but we didn't get the results back until after Chris was released. I could only hold him for the twenty-four hours, and once he made bail, he vanished." Dave hung his head, seeming to take the events as a personal failure.

"Why didn't you tell us before? What did Doc find?" Gabe asked. Suddenly things were becoming a bit clearer.

"I honestly thought we'd heard the last of Chris once he knew he had no chance with you." Dave rifled through the pages before finding the one he wanted and handed it to Gabe. "Doc found methamphetamine in his bloodwork at levels that indicate long-term use. I've issued a warrant for his arrest and contacted his sister over in Houston, but she stated she hadn't seen him in over a year and that he owed her money." He shook his head and his lip flattened out; this was the same woman that attempted to steal money from Gabe. "I asked Houston PD to check his apartment. Sure enough, it's empty and the neighbors stated no one's been seen there in months. DMV records indicate that Chris does own a silver Honda Accord."

"Shit…he can't actually believe I would take him back?" Gabe's frustration was rising by the second. How could Chris just disappear without someone seeing him?

"My best guess is money." Dad's deep voice sounded just as angry as Gabe's.

"Money? Why the hell would I give that man anything after what he did to me?" Gabe could now understand Chris's odd behavior. Meth was a dangerous and deadly drug, but why he thought to come to Gabe for money of all things was truly ludicrous.

"Chris isn't thinking clearly if he's still using. All he knows is that he needs money to buy drugs and the one person who he could count on for money was unfortunately you, Gabe. In my opinion he sees Johnny as competition." Gabe couldn't fault Dave's logic; after all, he was police chief for a reason.

"Now that we know what we're up against, we can be better prepared until Chris is arrested," Gabe said. "We'll move Jesse into one of the spare bedrooms, and I'm pretty sure Royce won't be too far behind, but we'll need help when Royce and I are at work. Johnny won't be able to do much with his burns still healing." Gabe threw out the beginnings of a plan. Soon his family chimed in and a schedule was set.

Dad decided to call an old Marine buddy of his, who now owned his own security firm out in Colorado, for help securing the interior of Gabe's home. Gabe would do whatever it took to keep his love safe. Nothing was off limits, including hiring armed security specialists.

When Royce and Johnny came back from visiting Jesse, Royce quickly made plans to move a few bags over to Gabe's house so that he could stay in the spare room attached to the one Jesse would be recovering in. Johnny was strangely quiet, barely giving any suggestions. Eventually, he simply curled up beside Gabe and fell asleep. Once a plan was in place, Royce decided to stay at the hospital with Jesse, and Gabe carried a still sleeping Johnny back to his truck and drove them home.

Johnny woke halfway home but remained quiet and reserved even as Gabe began to undress him in their bedroom. Once he had Johnny's shirt off, his love placed soft kisses across Gabe's bare chest. His warm, wet lips left a trail of goose bumps on Gabe's overheated flesh. Instinctively, he flexed his hips, rubbing his straining erection over Johnny's stomach.

"Johnny, your doctor said we shouldn't raise your rate of breathing very high while your lungs are still healing, and you haven't even begun to recover from your burns." Gabe was desperately trying to be the voice of reason, but Johnny wasn't having it. He responded by rubbing his hard, jean-covered cock against Gabe's thigh, moaning softly at the friction.

"Need you, Gabe. Need to feel you against me. Please?" Johnny's green eyes shone bright. His pupils were dilated and his face and chest were flushed red with desire. He was simply gorgeous.

Gabe knew then in that moment that he would do whatever Johnny wanted, but at the same time, he would ensure that he was safe. He'd wanted Johnny since the first moment he saw him, and sleeping together every night with him in his arms only heightened that need. He would still make sure Johnny's lungs and burns weren't further damaged, but Gabe would give Johnny the physical connection and love he so desperately needed.

He easily lifted Johnny to the bed and quickly stripped them both of their remaining clothing before blanketing Johnny with his own body. Deep, guttural groans filled the room as their cocks rubbed together for the first time. Johnny's hips bucked, urgently rutting himself against Gabe's muscled abdomen. Wet trails of precum laced the thick, dark hair covering Gabe's stomach leading down to his hard, pulsing cock.

"Easy, baby, I'll take care of you, but you have to lie back and let me give you what you need. I won't have you injuring yourself." Gabe pressed his large body down further onto Johnny, essentially pinning him to the bed, trapping him and making Johnny groan even louder... *Interesting.*

"Put your hands above your head, Johnny, and don't move them," Gabe ordered firmly, his dominant nature charging to the forefront. Johnny's beautiful, slim, cut penis twitched and oozed more precum from its swollen pink head as he quickly obeyed and waited for Gabe's next order. Johnny was absolutely perfect.

"You won't move until I tell you to. Do you understand?" Gabe kept his voice firm while running his hands up and down the toned sides of his lover's body, caressing over muscle and soft skin. "If you move, I'll have to tie you to the bed."

Johnny's quick intake of breath and dilated pupils were all the answer Gabe needed; Johnny liked that idea...a lot. "You want that, Johnny, don't you? You want to be tied up so you're at my mercy." Gabe punctuated his statement by capturing Johnny's right nipple in between his teeth and sucking it into his mouth, making Johnny arch his back off the mattress and cry out in pleasure.

"Yes...yes, please, Gabe." Johnny's begging ramped up Gabe's arousal to the point that he had to squeeze the base of his cock to stop from coming on the spot. He lost his control so easily around this man.

Gabe released Johnny's swollen, red nipple and began nibbling and kissing his way down his body, stopping to press his face into his lover's pale blond pubic hair and breathing in his musky, male scent. Gabe wanted to make love to Johnny so badly he could barely think straight, but he knew they couldn't do that just yet, not with Johnny's many healing injuries. But he could give himself and Johnny the release they both so badly needed. In one fluid movement, Gabe raised his head and sucked Johnny's cock down to the root while keeping both of his hands firmly on Johnny's hips, stopping him from moving and possibly injuring himself.

"Gabe!"

After that, Johnny began babbling incoherently between moans of pleasure while Gabe sucked and licked at an almost frenzied pace. The taste and feel of the man underneath him was intoxicating. All too soon, Gabe found himself on the edge again, knowing Johnny was just as close. Gabe raised his massive body up and brought their straining erections together. Capturing them both in his large hand, Gabe pumped his hand and hips, moving his painfully hard penis against Johnny's, their combined precum lubing his hand as he jacked them both.

Johnny's hips jerked violently, losing his rhythm, evidence of how close he was to coming. His beautiful green eyes never left Gabe's as his breathing hitched and he moaned Gabe's name loudly before he came. The intensity of the love they shared and the raw desire he felt watching Johnny come sent Gabe into his own orgasm so fast that he had no warning. Gabe roared his pleasure. His balls pulled tight, his muscles seized, and the head of his cock felt like it was exploding with wave after wave of his release.

Gabe was, thankfully, able to keep his weight off Johnny while he struggled to come back from one of the strongest orgasms he'd felt in a very long time, if ever. He nuzzled the side of Johnny's face, placing soft kisses along his jawline before playfully nipping at his ear. Gabe always felt loved and contented having Johnny in his arms, and now was no different.

Johnny laughed happily and finally brought his arms back down to wrap them around Gabe's neck. "I love you, Gabe."

"I love you so much, Johnny. I'm sorry about everything. I never expected—"

"No, none of this is your fault. None of it." Johnny voice was filled with anger, and even if Gabe understood it wasn't directed at him he still didn't like having his love this angry.

"Hold on, baby, let me get us cleaned up and tucked in. I want you comfortable. It's been one hell of a day for you." Gabe carefully stood, walked to their attached bathroom, cleaned himself quickly, and then warmed a soft washcloth for Johnny.

The sight of his Johnny lying naked, eyes closed with a happy smile on his face, touched Gabe and brought him a sense of peace. He took a moment to appreciate Johnny's sweaty, sated body glistening in the soft light from the bedside lamp. His soft, curly blond hair scattered wildly across the pillow shone like a halo and was absolutely breathtaking. Johnny looked every bit the angel he was—*a debauched angel*, Gabe chuckled to himself—but still his angel. That one image of his lover would forever be etched into his memory. He gently cleaned Johnny's softened cock and lightly furred stomach before tossing the cloth into the dirty laundry. After tucking a tired Johnny under the covers and turning off the lights, Gabe joined him.

Johnny lay with his head tucked safely in the nook between Gabe's neck and shoulder, half of his body on top of him. They fit together perfectly in Gabe's opinion. His love had been quiet for such a long time that he thought Johnny had fallen asleep and was a bit shocked when he spoke softly.

"We won't let him destroy what we have, Gabe." Johnny held him tight. His voice might have been muted, but it was firm. "I won't lose you."

Gabe hugged Johnny closer until he was lying fully on top of him, safely wrapped in his arms. "I love you so damn much, Johnny. I could never go back to a life without you. I'll protect you and our life together, baby. I won't give you up."

"Promise me, Gabe."

"Promise, baby."

Chapter Eight

The next five days were chaotic for Johnny; between his own physiotherapy sessions for his hands, he was also preparing a room to become Jesse's home away from home. Gabe and Royce had taken care of all the medical supplies that needed to be stocked while Johnny and the Mason women concentrated on the comforting, homey aspect. Johnny had to admit that he was beginning to feel more and more at home here every day. He felt like a Mason, and the family made sure he knew they considered him one as well.

Stacks of homemade frozen dinners and casseroles were stocked in a new chest freezer in the basement and every cupboard was crammed full. If Johnny didn't know better, he would think the women believed the four men would never be able to find a grocery store again. He loved this family so much.

Jesse had been more than understanding once they told him who had tried to run them down, and no matter how many times he or Gabe tried to apologize, Jesse refused to allow them to take any of the blame. Jesse had stated repeatedly that Chris was responsible for his own actions and that Jesse was just glad he'd been there to push Johnny out of the way. Jesse also stressed to Johnny that he was to always listen to his instincts like they did that day; it saved his life. Johnny swore to Jesse he would never doubt himself again.

When Royce told Jesse he would be staying with Gabe and Johnny so that he and the Mason family could take care of him, Johnny expected all hell to break loose. Thunderclouds appeared in Jesse's eyes and he opened his mouth as if to argue the point, but Royce simply gave Jesse a look that Johnny had never seen before on the quiet man's face. It stated flat out, "I'm in charge, and I dare you to fight me on this." Jesse wisely and quickly agreed to temporarily move in. After the first few days of the four of them living together, Johnny began to see and understand the new dynamic between Royce and Jesse.

Jesse might be the muscled, tattoo-covered biker and he might have sixty pounds on Royce, who was himself a large man to begin with, but Royce was fully in charge and the much more dominant of the two. Jesse was in fact a gentle giant who seemed to flourish under Royce's strong, dominant nature.

Royce had shown he was no one to be messed with when Jesse's brother randomly showed up at the hospital one day and tried to have Jesse transferred out of state. Jesse's terrified look caused Royce to step in and have the brother removed from the hospital.

Apparently Jesse had been running from his family for much the same reason as Johnny. Though Jesse's family spouted religion and sin, and Johnny's father's interests centered on money and reputation, both families evidently believed pain was the best method to get their sons to comply.

Sadly, one afternoon while Johnny, Gabe, Royce, and Mom were helping Jesse get ready to leave the hospital, they saw the evidence of his family's attempts at "reconditioning" their gay son littering Jesse's brutalized back. Long, jagged scars covered almost every inch of skin. Royce quickly covered them before Jesse could realize anyone had seen his pain, and the family carried on as if they saw nothing. Johnny swore he would be there for his new friend if Jesse ever wanted to talk to him and would personally kick Jesse's brother's ass if he came near him again...okay, maybe Johnny would have Gabe kick the evil man's ass, but the intention was still the same.

Royce doted on Jesse, and Jesse soaked it up like a sponge. It was easy for anyone to see he had been starving for affection. Clem had assured Jesse that he would still have a job once he was healed enough to work again. Sadly, the doctors thought that would be months away at the very least.

All in all, everything was moving relatively smoothly right up until ten seconds before, when Johnny came out of the house to get the morning paper only to find the tires on his car had been slashed.

"Gabe!" Johnny screamed in fear as he began backing up toward the house while scanning the front yard, half-expecting Chris to jump out at any minute.

Gabe came barreling out of the house in only a pair of jeans. Royce was close behind carrying a baseball bat. Gabe snagged Johnny around the waist and led him back inside the house while Royce took a closer look at his car.

"What's wrong?" Jesse asked as he steered his wheelchair into the kitchen where Gabe sat Johnny on the counter and reached for his phone.

He handed the phone to Jesse before answering. "Call the police station, Jesse. Tell them Johnny's car has been vandalized and to send an officer out. I want both of you to stay here in the kitchen while Royce and I have a look around." Gabe kissed Johnny quickly and walked back out the door.

Jesse called the station and a deputy was on his way over. Johnny also saw Dante Snow's black SUV pull in. He was the scary-looking security professional that Dad's old military buddy had sent to help find Chris. So far, Chris was still out there somewhere, even after Dante and the police had found Chris's car and the room he'd been renting in the neighboring county. They all thought he would be caught soon. He had no vehicle or place to sleep, and every law enforcement officer in the surrounding counties was looking for him. Dante had installed security cameras around the house and an expensive security system to cover the interior. Johnny just hoped they had caught Chris on tape slashing his tires.

"It'll be okay, Johnny." Jesse gently took hold of Johnny's shaking, bandaged hands. Until then, he hadn't even noticed he was shaking.

"I guess knowing Chris was this close to the house has me a little rattled." Johnny tried to calm down, but with every passing second, it was getting harder and harder to breathe. *Shit.* Johnny knew the signs; he needed his inhaler, but for the life of him he couldn't remember where it was. Gabe would be pissed. Johnny had been caught a few times without it when he couldn't catch his breath, but dammit he was only going to the driveway for the stupid newspaper this time.

"Johnny! Johnny, what do you need?" Jesse asked and started yelling for Gabe and Royce.

"In-inhale—" Johnny tried to get the words out, but he didn't have enough air. His vision was dimming fast as tiny pinpricks of light sparkled in front of him.

Suddenly, Johnny was lifted from the counter and the plastic of his inhaler was pushed to his lips. "Breathe in, Johnny. Come on, baby, just take a breath in." Gabe's voice pleaded as Johnny struggled to get some air and his medication into his lungs.

Minutes passed by slowly, but, bit by bit, Johnny managed to get more and more medication into his lungs and his breathing became less labored. Gabe had him cuddled safely in his arms on one of the living room couches. Royce, Jesse, and Dante were still in the kitchen giving them some privacy.

"Easy, Johnny." Gabe spoke softly, letting Johnny burrow a bit deeper into his embrace. "I've got you, but from now on, you're going to carry your inhaler in every damn piece of clothing you have. There'll be one in every room and I'll tie one on a damn chain around your neck if I have to."

Johnny could only nod in agreement even though they both knew that plan wasn't practical. He'd been scared enough times when he'd been unable to catch his breath, and he could still feel Gabe's body tremor underneath him in fear.

"How many do you want?" Royce asked from the kitchen. Johnny and Gabe both looked up to see Royce with his cell phone in one hand while his other ran through Jesse's hair, soothing the man. "The pharmacy has to order more in if you want over ten."

"Five should be a good start. I want Johnny to have one near him at all times, and if that means everyone in the family carries one, then I'm good with that," Gabe answered and Royce went back to his call.

"I don't need family to carry my inhaler, Gabe. I'm completely capable of carrying my own damn inhaler. Just because I've misplaced it a few times doesn't mean you get to treat me like a child." Johnny cringed. He didn't know where all his anger was coming from, but it was coming on fast. "I'm an adult, fully capable of making my own decisions. I've been doing it for years before you came along. Just because I'm injured doesn't mean I've lost the ability to think rationally. I'm a capable person. This isn't permanent. I will get my life back!" *Oh shit!* Johnny was beginning to feel like a child, and he didn't like it very much.

"Johnny, I know you can take care of yourself, but please understand this is something I need to do, sweetheart. I don't think any less of you or that you aren't capable, but you knew my need to be in control and to have you safe right from the beginning. I can't change that, Johnny. I love you, and by letting me take care of you, you're helping to keep me sane."

"Keep you sane?" Johnny huffed. He knew Gabe was trying to make him feel better about his inability to keep track of his inhaler and the fact that he might never be able to use his hands the same way again, but keeping him sane was a bit of a stretch. The love he saw in those brown eyes was always his undoing, but today he was just too damn frustrated to care.

"Yes, Johnny. Hell, if anything happened to you, it would push me over the edge. That is the God's honest truth." Gabe's voice wavered, and Johnny began to understand that, by keeping himself safe, he was making Gabe content and calm. This was something his bear of a man needed to be happy, and Johnny would give him anything if he could.

"Fine, Gabe. I know you're only trying to keep me safe, but sometimes I feel like you don't even trust me to do that on my own. I feel like I'm being patronized. I'd have hoped that you realized by now that I'm a grown man." Johnny hoped to lighten the mood a bit, fearing he might have overreacted.

"Oh, I've noticed." Gabe's voice dipped low as he nuzzled the curly blond mess on top of Johnny's head, making Johnny realize he hadn't even had a shower yet. "And I'm sorry if I've ever made you feel that way, Johnny. It's just, with everything that's happened in the past few weeks, I need to know I've done everything I can to make sure the people that I love are safe. I trust you with everything I am; I never thought I would be able to do that ever again, Johnny. You've given me my peace of mind back, and I want to share everything with you." Gabe always sounded so excited when he spoke about their future, and Johnny desperately wanted to let his fears over Chris slip away, if only for a little while.

Over the past few weeks, they both had bared their souls and let the other in so completely that Johnny felt they'd known each other for years, not weeks. Though Johnny knew he loved Gabe without question and wanted to spend the rest of his life with the man, he feared all his happiness would be ripped away at any moment. He knew it was due to Chris and, once he was caught, Johnny would feel more secure, but as of this moment, Johnny felt anything but secure knowing Chris had been within feet of the house.

"Do you think it was Chris?" Johnny asked Dante as he, Jesse, and Royce joined them in the living room.

Dante placed his laptop on the coffee table and turned the monitor to face the group. "Yes, I'm afraid it was indeed Chris," Dante confirmed while the image on the screen displayed a thin, dishevelled-looking man viciously stabbing a long, serrated knife into Johnny's tires.

The room went silent as Chris went about, almost joyfully, from one tire to the next with a look of absolute bliss on his face. Johnny felt the cold chill of fear race through his body, causing him to shake slightly.

"That's enough. We've seen enough." Gabe gently tucked Johnny's head back into his nook and away from the laptop. Out of the corner of his eye, Johnny could see Royce comforting a pale Jesse much the same way. How could he have forgotten that Jesse was a victim of this lunatic as well?

"Are you okay, Jesse?" Johnny asked, his voice breaking slightly.

"Yes, I'll be fine. It was just a bit of a shock seeing him again after the last time. He…he had that same look on his face. It's like a fucked-up, gleeful rage. I…I just…" Jesse answered softly, leaning a bit further into Royce's chest.

"I've got you." Royce folded Jesse into his arms; Jesse was visibly shaking by now.

"I'm calling in Spider. He'll find that bastard." A clearly agitated Dante stormed out of the house, stabbing his big fingers onto his phone's screen as he left. "Spider, it's Snow. I've got a job for you."

*****

Gabe helped Johnny from his truck and into a nondescript brick building that was causing Gabe an amazing amount of stress, but he was able to hold it securely under wraps for now. He was proud he was able to keep his hand from shaking and placed it possessively on Johnny's lower back before leading his love to the second floor. He had been planning this for weeks and hoped this would do the trick. Since Chris's little overnight visit six nights ago, Johnny had seemed much more subdued and quiet. Gabe didn't like it one bit. His Johnny was full of life. Even with his injuries, he would be humming around the house or out in the gardens. Chris wasn't going to take that from Johnny; Gabe wouldn't allow it.

"Are you going to tell me why we're here, Gabe?" Johnny asked softly. They made their way down the long, wood-panelled hallway, Johnny glued to Gabe's side.

"Not quite yet, baby. It'll just be a few more minutes." Gabe prayed he'd made the right decision and wasn't pushing Johnny too far too fast or this could bite him in the ass. "It wouldn't be much of a surprise if I told you, right?"

"I promise to act surprised." Johnny giggled and gave him the best damn puppy-dog eyes Gabe had seen since his baby niece. Gabe felt his heart lighten just a bit with the return of his playful Johnny; he wanted him to be happy. Johnny had given Gabe the most precious of gifts—peace. Since Chris, Gabe had been living day to day, tied up in knots without ever considering the future. His trust issues kept him firmly rooted in the past. Now his future lay before him, full of possibilities, full of love, full of the kind, gentle man beside him. Gabe considered himself a very lucky man.

"Not going to happen, baby. Besides, we're here." Gabe smiled and ushered Johnny into the office at the end of the hall.

Johnny walked hesitantly into the waiting area. Appearing unsure of what to do, he turned his questioning eyes up to Gabe. "Just take a seat, Johnny, and I'll let them know we've arrived."

Gabe quickly checked in with the receptionist before rejoining Johnny, who was sitting rigidly in the old, plastic waiting room chairs. "Johnny, I would never take you any place where you need to be frightened." He spoke calmly while rubbing soothing circles onto Johnny's back. Gabe had learned during their time together just how to calm his lover when he became tense or upset.

"Of course you wouldn't! I trust you completely, Gabe. I'm sorry if I made you feel that way. I know you would never put me in harm's way. I love you." Johnny spoke with such conviction in his voice that Gabe's heart beat just a bit faster with the love he felt for the man in his arms. "It's just that I keep expecting him to show up at any moment. I…"

Johnny immediately lowered his eyes and worried his bottom lip. Hearing him voice his concerns brought out Gabe's protective instincts and he gathered Johnny further into the shelter of his arms. Sometimes the depth of love he felt for Johnny would steal his breath and nearly knock him on his ass. This shy, brave man was Gabe's future. Everything that he had ever wanted and dreamed of was wrapped up in his arms at that moment.

"I'll do whatever it takes to protect you, Johnny. He'll have to go through me to get to you." Gabe tried to reassure Johnny, knowing every word he spoke was the absolute truth.

"That's what I'm afraid of. Look at what happened to Jesse; he was hurt trying to protect me. Who else is going to get hurt while Chris is trying to get to me? I can't handle the thought of that happening to anyone else." Johnny's confession hit Gabe hard. His Johnny wasn't concerned with the danger to himself. Gabe should have known this inherently good man wouldn't be selfish, even when faced with a psychotic man's rage. "If he showed up, you could be injured, Gabe, or the family. I couldn't live with it if anyone else got hurt."

"Oh, baby, don't worry about me. Chris won't get the chance. You've seen Spider; that man is truly scary." Johnny's eyes widened before he nodded his head in agreement.

To say the man Dante had called in to search for Chris was intense would be such a huge understatement. It would be as foolish as saying a world war was a slight disagreement. Thankfully, Dante had warned everyone before he'd arrived or Spider might have caused quite a few suspicious-persons calls into the police station. The huge man had eyes as dark as his black hair and he stood at least 6'5" tall with muscles hard-earned from years in the service and constant assignments around the world. After hearing a few stories passed through Dante, Gabe wasn't surprised to find out that Spider was a decorated war hero, having saved four other Marines from capture and leading them back to safety after their Cobra helicopter was shot down over Afghanistan.

In truth, even with his scary-ass exterior, Spider hadn't been anything other than respectful toward everyone. He was a former Marine turned security specialist/bodyguard working freelance with Dante for years, still protecting those who couldn't protect themselves. He and Dante had heightened security around the house, set up motion sensors, and secured the neighborhood, with all the neighbors' blessings of course. Again, thank God for small towns.

He helped elderly Mrs. Rose down the street carry her groceries into her home and then sat for tea. This last one seemed odd, but the man was a walking contradiction. Spider's presence caused people to pause; he exuded a lethal strength that made people not want to step a toe out of line. All Gabe cared about was that the man continued to use an almost gentle nature when dealing with Johnny, Jesse, or any of the Masons he'd met. Gabe knew Spider would turn into a lethal predator when he needed to protect the people Gabe loved, of that there was no doubt.

Grandma Rose seemed to just love the mountain of a man and had invited him out with the rest of the White Hair Crew. The sight of this huge, admittedly deadly man sitting at a table in Ms. Stephanie's bakery surrounded by elderly woman eating pastries and having tea would be forever etched in everyone's memory. You just don't see that shit every day.

"Mr. Jeffrey?" a young woman said softly and smiled toward them from the now opened doorway.

Johnny stood with Gabe and followed the woman into the back offices. Johnny's eyes were wide and hadn't stopped moving from one machine to another once they went through the doors. Gabe didn't even bother trying to figure out what half of the machines surrounding him did, but if they helped Johnny, he would gladly learn.

"Gabe?" Johnny's voice was just above a whisper when the woman stopped in front of a rather impressive-looking computer system with all kinds of bells and whistles. Again, Gabe had no idea what he was truly looking at beyond the keyboard and screen.

To give the young woman credit, she hadn't said a word. Gabe had told Mr. Parks, the owner of Parks Adaptive Devices, that this was a surprise for Johnny, and by the way that Johnny stood stone-still Gabe wondered if he had just made a huge mistake. He had wanted to give Johnny some of his freedom back and knew he had loved his job in graphic design before the fire had destroyed his hands. According to Josie and several others, Johnny was very accomplished and sought after by companies requiring his flair for design and original ideas.

"Johnny, I...," Gabe began to play with the hem of his white button-down shirt as the silence dragged on. Johnny turned around to face Gabe with tears streaming down his face. "I'm sorry. I thought—"

Whatever he was going to say was silenced when Johnny threw himself into Gabe's arms and began kissing him as if his very life depended on it. Only the soft giggles of the forgotten young woman stopped Johnny from full-out mauling Gabe. Johnny blushed beautifully when he pulled away to look at the table again.

"It's...it's amazing. I never dreamed, Gabe." Johnny began to touch each piece of machinery almost reverently with a look of awe on his face.

The patient young woman finally spoke. "I'm Becky. It's an honor to meet you, Johnny."

"I'm sorry, an honor?" Johnny asked, stopping his perusal for a moment.

The woman stepped a little closer to Johnny and Gabe almost felt silly when his protectiveness brought him to Johnny's side. As if the small woman was a threat, but Gabe couldn't turn it off if he wanted to, which he didn't.

The young woman simply smiled and, with great care, lightly touched Johnny's bandaged hands; there was sadness in her eyes. "I'm Janice's baby sister. You saved my sister's life in that fire."

A tear slid down Becky's cheek and Johnny immediately wrapped his arms around her, crooning softly as she cried on Johnny's uninjured shoulder. Gabe had no idea that Janice's sister worked here when he stopped by to inquire on the system, but the day was just full of surprises. After a few minutes, Becky got her emotions back under control and gave Johnny a watery smile while drying her eyes.

"Thank you, Johnny. I wish I could take away your pain, but at least I can help you with your surprise." Becky waved her arms over Johnny's new adaptive technology computer system. Gabe had been guaranteed it had all the necessary equipment to help Johnny return to his love of graphic design.

"You did this for me?" Johnny turned to Gabe, his eyes still red and puffy, and his voice wavered slightly.

Gabe pulled Johnny into his arms and nuzzled the side of his neck like he knew Johnny loved, and just as expected, he arched his neck to give Gabe more room. "I know how much you loved your job, baby, and since you don't currently have one to go back to, I thought if you had the right equipment, you might like taking on a few projects from home. Not that you need to work if you don't want to. I just want you to be happy."

Gabe didn't want Johnny to feel obligated to work. Gabe could easily take care of both of them, but he had the feeling his lover would never be comfortable with that.

"It's a breathtaking system, Gabe. Thank you. It's perfect, but…" Johnny's voice trailed off as he lifted his injured hands, the defeat as evident in his voice as on his face.

"That's why Gabe came to us," Becky stated cheerfully, while carrying another box full of parts that reminded him of game controllers of some sort toward them. "We get to customize this bad boy so that you can work with as few limitations as possible. Even if your hands don't regain their full mobility or strength, we can adapt the system to your needs."

Johnny chewed his bottom lip and looked at the system, as if afraid of it. Gabe didn't like that look at all. "Baby, what's wrong?" Gabe held Johnny a little tighter from behind, trying to lend his strength to his love.

"What if we try and it doesn't work? What if my hands are too messed up? What if I can never be normal again?" Johnny released a few of his fears in a flood of emotions that Gabe felt had been bottled up since the fire. Gabe thanked whoever was listening that he was here when Johnny finally was able to voice some of those fears.

"You've already gained back more feeling than you thought you would, and the doctors believe that, with continued therapy, you'll get up to 80 percent of your range of motion back. We'll do whatever it takes for you to feel as normal as you can. I know it won't be easy for you, and it'll take time, but I'll be there every step of the way. I promise you won't have to go through this alone, ever. I love you." Gabe held Johnny, waiting for him to make his choice about the computer system. They could leave now and Gabe would support his decision.

With one final nuzzle, Johnny bravely pulled away and joined Becky at the desk. He knew that in the past, Johnny viewed himself as weak at times. His history had forced him to believe this as truth. But anyone who met Johnny could see his strength and determination shine through, and over the past few weeks Gabe believed Johnny had begun to see it, too. Gabe moved back to lean against the wall and watched as she showed him something that reminded Gabe of a joystick he used to play video games with as a child. She began measuring Johnny's hands, then recorded his grip strength from another machine, while yet another checked his range of motion. Becky had him attempt to use the keyboard and a few other machines while she took notes on what Johnny could and couldn't manipulate with his hands.

Once done, she brought out a few adaptive devices and began to mount them temporarily on a few machines. She removed the keyboard altogether and replaced it with a touch pad covered in symbols and an attached thick-handled stylus, which Johnny used to touch those symbols. Also, she brought out a small microphone and attached it to the system. Then she asked Johnny to speak clearly into it as she programmed the necessary software.

Gabe stood in amazement as, in just over two hours, Becky managed to have Johnny working on a basic mock-up system with multiple temporary devices as his aids. Gabe knew it would take a few sessions for Johnny to feel confident using his new system, but from all indications, he was off to a good start. Johnny's smile stretched from ear to ear as the screen came to life and he navigated through the various programs. Every few minutes, Johnny would turn his head and search out Gabe to make sure he could see what Johnny had accomplished. Gabe simply smiled with pride at the resilience Johnny possessed; he never gave up. No matter how afraid he was to fail, Johnny pushed himself forward. Gabe wasn't sure if he deserved a man like Johnny, but he wasn't foolish enough to ever let him go.

"I believe that's about all I need to get started on this first round of changes, Johnny." Becky set her clipboard down and turned to Gabe. "I'll need you two to come back in about a week from now to try out all the modifications. I'll call you to confirm an appointment time."

"Thank you for doing all of this for me, Becky." Johnny stood and stretched the stiffness out of his back. His shirt rode up slightly, revealing the toned muscles of Johnny's abdomen, and Gabe's cock took notice and began to swell. Gabe quickly adjusted his stance so that his need for Johnny remained hidden in such a public place before he joined him by the door. Gabe desperately wanted to touch every inch of Johnny and make love to him for hours, but he held himself in check day after day until given the all clear by his doctors.

"It's my pleasure, Johnny. Don't worry, we'll get you all set up in no time at all," Becky assured and then led them back out to the front offices.

They said their good-byes and headed out into the Texas heat. Gabe kept Johnny tucked securely into his side, eyes scanning the area instinctively, looking for any and all threats. After lifting Johnny into his seat and buckling the seatbelt, Gabe kissed him deeply, exploring his mouth freely. After several enjoyable minutes later, Gabe finally broke away, allowing them both to breathe. The dazed expression in his lover's eyes stroked Gabe's ego just a bit, and he wanted to make it his mission to give Johnny that look every damn day.

"I'm so proud of you, Johnny. That took a lot of courage. How do you feel?" Gabe wanted to make sure Johnny was truly fine with today's events.

Johnny closed his eyes and took a few moments to gather his thoughts before he answered, and when he did, the love shining in his eyes just about floored Gabe. "You've given me back a part of myself that I thought would be lost. A part of myself that I had fought so hard to have away from my father. I—I can never truly explain to you what today has meant to me, Gabe. Everything I come up with doesn't seem strong enough a word for what I feel right now. 'Thank you' doesn't seem to be enough for everything you've done to help put my life back together. I love you, Gabe. I can't imagine ever being without you."

"And you'll never have to, baby." Gabe leaned in for another kiss, but the shrill blast of a horn cut through their peaceful bubble.

Gabe turned ready to tear a strip off whoever was behind them, until he looked up and saw a panicked Lee behind the wheel of his own truck. Gabe immediate went on alert, scanning the area again before he shut his truck door, instructing Johnny to remain inside, and quickly approached his friend and teammate.

Lee already had his window down and began talking even before Gabe made it to his door. "We have to get to the hospital. Frank's already there!"

"What? What's wrong? What happened to Frank?" Gabe's words came tumbling out of his mouth, fear that something had happened to his best friend's husband making the words blend together.

"No, he's okay. It's Lucy. She's in labor; the baby's coming. My son and your godson, let's move!" Gabe could tell Lee was almost in a panic. Lucy, Lee and Frank's amazing surrogate, was due over a week ago, but it finally looked like the little guy was ready to finally come out and meet his fathers.

"Okay, but park your truck over there beside mine, man. You can't drive like this. I'll take you to the hospital." Gabe pointed to the open parking spot and turned away from Lee, sure that his friend would follow his instructions.

Johnny's head was turned almost all the way around in his truck, trying to watch Gabe's approach, but he hadn't attempted to get out, which made Gabe eternally grateful. Until Chris was caught, Johnny's safety was first and foremost in his thoughts. He opened the driver's door just as Lee jumped into the backseat, eyes bright with nerves and excitement.

"Is everything okay?" Johnny asked, turning around to face Lee.

"I'm having a baby—no, Lucy's having the baby. She's in labor." Lee looked ready to throw up as Gabe pulled back onto the road, turning toward the hospital.

Johnny was just about vibrating out of his seat with excitement. "That's amazing, Lee. Congratulations."

Lee's returning smile was so big, Gabe had to wonder if it hurt his face. He was the picture of happiness. Gabe allowed himself a brief moment to imagine himself and Johnny in this situation. They had discussed having children. Gabe believed in absolute honesty going in and wanted to make sure the man he wanted in his life actually wanted children as much as he did. Thankfully, by the way Johnny's eyes lit up at the mere mention of having children, Gabe knew even before Johnny confirmed his suspicions that he did indeed wish to be a father.

A family—his family—and Johnny would be its center, just as he was now Gabe's home. Together they would build a future. Gabe reached over, taking Johnny's hand and kissing it gently. The happiness on Johnny's face added to Gabe's own joy.

My family.

Chapter Nine

Just over four hours later, Lucy delivered a healthy, seven-pound-six-ounce baby boy. Both mom and baby were doing great, and Johnny was beside himself with excitement as Sam led him and Gabe down to their room. It was early evening by now and the hospital was quieting down for the night—well, everyone else was quieting down for the evening except for the adorable, red-faced screaming bundle in Frank's arms. The look of complete adoration on Frank's face was serene compared to the panic-stricken Lee.

"Sweetheart, sit down before you fall down. Our son is fine; he's simply hungry," Frank whispered before placing a bottle to their son's searching mouth, and quiet descended.

Lee seemed to finally realize that Johnny, Gabe, and Sam were standing in the doorway. He quickly came over and hugged all three. "Come in and meet our son, Jacob Samuel Rogers."

Lee took position behind his husband who was now rocking the sleepy little bundle of blue. Lee's pride and love seemed to fill the room, causing Johnny to quickly blink back tears of joy for the two new fathers. Lucy lay comfortably surrounded by pillows and flowers, smiling happily from her hospital bed as she watched Frank and Lee bond with their new baby. After Johnny had met the woman for lunch weeks ago, he swore she was an angel sent to his new friends. She selflessly helped give the greatest gift possible—life, and thus created a new family.

Lucy had also made Johnny and Gabe an offer that left him speechless. When the time was right, she would gladly become their surrogate as well. Johnny had not known at the time, but Lee and Frank had set up the lunch date with that one specific purpose in mind. Lucy had heard about their story and wished to meet Johnny and Gabe to see if they fit and, according to her, they did. She had stated quite plainly that if she felt a couple could not or would not love their child with everything they had, then she would not give them that chance. Lucy was convinced, even with Johnny's injuries, that they would make a loving and happy family for any child lucky enough to have them. Johnny had never been more thankful for the generosity of others than he was at that very moment.

"He's so beautiful," Johnny sighed, his voice cracking slightly with emotion. "Welcome to the world, Jacob. Your daddies love you very much."

Gabe ran his huge, comforting hand up and down Johnny's back, speaking softly to Lee, but Johnny couldn't take his eyes off the tiny sleeping bundle. He was perfect.

"Do you want to hold him, Johnny?" Frank asked.

Johnny was excited for all of a few seconds before his smile fell and he remembered his damaged hands. "I don't think it's safe with my hands. I don't have much strength yet, and I don't want anything to happen." Johnny felt the disappointment like a physical blow. *What if I can't even hold my own children? What if I can't take care of them?*

Gabe must have felt his distress and was guiding Johnny toward a chair. "If you sit down, you'll be able to cradle him in your arms and I'll be right here."

Frank carefully laid Jacob into Johnny's waiting arms and Gabe crouched down in front of them both. Entranced, they sat, cooing and babbling nonsense to the now fully awake baby staring back at them.

The hours flew by and too soon it was time to leave Lucy and the new family for the night. Johnny was so overcome with emotions he actually shed tears before he gave the little bundle back to Lee, who smiled knowingly toward Gabe.

"I don't think it will be long before the two of you start having little ones of your own," Lee commented before laying Jacob in his bassinet beside Lucy.

Gabe looked at Johnny with such love that it made it hard to breathe, but this time he didn't need his inhaler; all he needed was Gabe. "Yes, I think once everything is settled, that will be something to consider."

Johnny was so thankful. All he had ever wanted was a family of his own to shower with all the love he had been saving up living with his taciturn father. He would give just about anything to have that, and he would fight tooth and nail to keep it.

Johnny took the opportunity to wiggle away, while Gabe and Lee made plans, and found the nearest washroom, with Sam in tow of course. Gabe would not allow him to be alone anywhere, not even a public washroom. Johnny didn't mind truly; he knew the dangers, had seen them firsthand and was in no hurry to experience them again.

"So, any news on the disappearing Chris?" Sam asked as he followed Johnny into the huge, eight-stall washroom. Large windows covered in an opaque film graced one wall, lighting up the entire room.

"Nothing since my tires were slashed. I'm getting really tired of that jerk."

"I don't blame you, Johnny. I don't imagine you'll ever feel safe until he's caught," Sam agreed with what Johnny himself had been feeling.

"I can't wait until he's in a nice, secure mental institution drooling all over himself." Johnny wasn't typically a spiteful person, but he was making an exception in this case.

Sam was laughing when Johnny came over to wash his hands, which wasn't easy with the few bandages that remained. "Well, there's the spitfire I know and love. Don't let that asshole have the satisfaction of causing you and Gabe any problems."

"Oh no, I won't. Gabe is mine, and I'll fight for him," Johnny assured Sam. He wasn't giving Gabe up no matter what happened.

"How 'bout we do that right now, you little homewrecker." The scratchy voice sounded almost painful, but when both Johnny and Sam turned to see Chris standing in the washroom doorway with a knife in his hand, Johnny's own voice failed and his vision dimmed for a moment.

Chris took a single step forward and Sam began backing up, putting himself in front of Johnny. No way would he allow that. Instead, Johnny grabbed a long-handled industrial broom left in the corner by the cleaning staff and stepped up beside Sam. It didn't matter that his hands were screaming in pain at even the loose grip he had on the steel handle; he wasn't going to let Chris hurt one more person. Johnny was done being prey to people who thought he was weak. Years of fear seemed to melt away, leaving a confident, stronger Johnny in its place.

At seeing Johnny's "weapon," Sam spun and grabbed the mop left in the same corner and crouched low, waiting for the first blow. The way Sam was positioning himself, Johnny knew he'd had some self-defense training, and Johnny decided then and there, once this was over, he was joining up for a class.

"Chris, you have to stop this. You're not thinking clearly," Sam tried to reason with the clearly agitated man. Chris's eyes were wild, the whites streaked red, giving him an almost possessed look. His clothes were streaked with what looked like mud and ripped in several places, causing Johnny to wonder if he'd been sleeping in the woods.

His hand shook as he lifted the lethal-looking blade directly toward Johnny. "That little bastard took my man, and he has to go. Then everything can go back to the way it was."

"You left Gabe, Chris. There's nothing for you to come back to." Sam was still attempting logic, but by the look in Chris's eyes, there wasn't a chance in hell logic was making it through Chris's delusion.

"He'll forgive me. Gabe loves me!" Chris hissed and took another step forward, confirming Johnny's original assumption.

"We're in a hospital, Chris. How do you even think you're going to get away with this?" Johnny had to try and keep him talking. Gabe would realize Johnny had been gone too long and come looking for him.

"It doesn't matter. Once you're gone, everything will be perfect again." Chris barked the words out, causing spittle to fly out of his mouth.

Obviously, what was left of his sanity was slipping away fast, and Chris lunged forward. Sam slammed the mop across Chris's head while Johnny brought the handle of his broom down on his arm, trying to dislodge the knife. Unfortunately, Chris only stumbled back but kept hold of the knife. The drugs in his system, obviously dulling the pain, allowed him to just keep on coming no matter how many times they hit him.

Shit, now what?

*****

Gabe was beginning to wonder what was taking Johnny and Sam so long when Dante and Spider came barreling into the room. Lee and Frank stood protectively in front of Lucy and their baby, sensing something was wrong.

"Where's Johnny?" Dante asked, he scanned the room and Gabe went on alert.

"In the washroom with Sam. What's going on?" Gabe answered but was already heading for the door; he had to find Johnny now.

"We tracked Chris to the hospital. He's in the building," Spider announced as he moved alongside Gabe.

Shit! Gabe took off at a dead run with Dante and Spider right behind him. Gabe's fear and adrenaline caused him to almost tear the washroom door off its hinges, but what he found on the other side was truly terrifying. Sam lay on the floor, attempting to get back on his feet, while holding his hand across a gash in his left thigh. Johnny was standing over him protectively while using a broom handle to dodge the knife Chris was wielding. Johnny's grip on the handle was slipping due to his injured hands. There was blood streaked on the floor and walls and, other than Sam's obvious wound, Gabe wasn't entirely certain where it was all coming from.

The sound of the door crashing open alerted Chris to their arrival, and without a second thought, he rushed past Johnny and Sam, lifted a waist-high steel garbage can, and threw it through the window.

Before Chris jumped out, he turned to Gabe and screamed. "You're mine! I'll kill anyone who tries to take my place!"

Dante and Spider had pulled out their guns, but the area was too confined and the odds of hitting Johnny and Sam too great to take the chance of firing.

"You have no place with me, Chris. You come near Johnny or my family again, and I'll kill you myself!" Gabe swore as he ran to help Johnny and Sam. Chris quickly jumped through the now-empty pane of glass and onto an adjoining roof, followed closely by Dante and Spider.

"Gabe, we have to get Sam help," Johnny cried while putting more pressure on Sam's bleeding leg wound.

Gabe ran for the door, still surprised no one had come to check on the noise, and yelled for help. This time, when he returned to Johnny's side, he saw the open wound on the back of Johnny's right arm. Grabbing a stack of paper towels from the dispenser, he pushed them up against Johnny's injury to try and slow the flow of blood.

"Just hold on, Sam. Help is on the way," Gabe assured, while having Johnny lean his weight back against him because he was beginning to shake.

"No worries, cuz. We did more damage to that asshole than he did to us, eh, Johnny?" Sam spoke through gritted teeth, his pain evident to Gabe.

"Damn right! He won't make the mistake of thinking he can take us on again." Johnny's words came out strong and sure, even though he was shaking like a leaf.

Spider came back through the window he had previously jumped out of and knelt beside Sam. "Hey, how ya doing, Sam?"

"Oh, you know, just getting off shift, wondering whether to get Thai or Greek for dinner—you?" Sam chuckled softly before laying his head back down onto the floor. Gabe could hear footsteps running down the hall toward them. Spider stood, pulled out his Glock, and put his body between the door and the three on the ground. Gabe refused to let go of the towels he had pressed against Johnny's wound, and Johnny was not letting go of Sam's leg, so it was up to Spider to protect the three of them in case Chris doubled back.

Dr. Green, Nurse Rouse, and two other nurses ran into the room and stopped dead in their tracks when they got a look at Spider standing ready to take on all comers. It took everyone mere seconds to realize there was no threat here, and Spider turned back to Sam.

"Dammit, Spider, you scared the heck outta me!" Nurse Rouse yelled before pushing past the huge man.

"Help them please, Nurse Rouse. The police are on their way," he asked before he ran his hand gently down Sam's pale cheek. That was the one thing about Spider; he was always a contradiction. He looked scary as hell and was ready to kill to protect them, but then spoke gently and politely to Nurse Rouse. "I'll be back. The three of us will get Thai for tonight." Sam simply smiled as Spider stood to leave. Gabe had no idea the two men even knew each other past the fact that Sam was Gabe's cousin and he absently wondered who the third person might be.

"Did you catch him?" Gabe asked as he moved out of one of the nurse's way while she wrapped Johnny's arm so they could be moved to the ER.

"No, he jumped down onto an adjoining roof and into the parking garage where he carjacked a woman before we could get near him. Dante and the police are searching for the car."

"Is the woman okay?" Johnny asked as Gabe gathered him into his arms so Sam could be loaded onto a gurney.

"Yes. She was just shaken up. She was parking her car and Chris grabbed the keys and took off. I'll be back." With a final look at Sam, Spider left—out of the door this time.

"Okay, let's move." Dr. Green took off through the door with the gurney while Nurse Rouse held Johnny's injured arm. Gabe scooped Johnny up when his legs finally gave out as his adrenaline began to crash.

"Gabe, w-w-why am I shaking?" Johnny asked through his chattering teeth.

"It's okay, baby. It's the adrenaline and shock. We'll get you to the ER and they'll fix you right up." Gabe would accept nothing less.

"Don't leave me." Now that the danger was over, Johnny's voice seemed almost fragile to Gabe, and he wished he could go out and find Chris to rip the man apart himself.

"I'm not going anywhere." Gabe carried Johnny into an ER bay alongside Nurse Rouse who was still applying pressure to his bleeding wound.

Dr. Green stayed with Sam while Dr. MacGuire came in to assess Johnny. Twenty-six stitches later and Johnny lay sleeping on the hospital bed, the day's events having finally caught up with him. Gabe sat quietly in a chair just staring at his love, the terror of the day hitting home. He once again could have lost Johnny so easily tonight. They had been lucky, and he would never make this mistake again. Gabe would hire a personal bodyguard for Johnny until this was over. He wasn't going to risk the man who meant everything to him.

Family had been in and out between Johnny and Sam's rooms for hours, but it was well past 1:00 a.m., and now only Sam's parents, Uncle Jack, Aunt Jane, Gabe, Ellen, and the chief remained. Two deputies had been assigned to keep watch over the two injured men. Sam had to have surgery to repair an artery damaged by

Chris's blade and would recover, but the wound would leave a substantial scar. Sam quickly brushed the news away, stating that this would only add character among his many tattoos. Dave and the rest of his deputies were searching alongside Dante and Spider, but they had yet to call with any news.

Gabe couldn't help but worry how Johnny was going to take this latest attack. The guilt Gabe alone was feeling was excruciating. He just hoped Johnny wouldn't take the actions of an obviously insane man as his own responsibility. Hell, if anyone was responsible for this mess, Gabe knew it was he himself.

"Son." Roger stood in the open doorway, his face a blank mask. "Your mom brought coffee. Let's go for a walk."

"I can't leave him, Dad." Gabe was nowhere near ready enough to leave Johnny.

"I know, son." Ellen walked in carrying her bag-o-tricks, as the kids used to call it. Seriously, Mom had everything in that oversized purse. "I'll sit with Johnny while you go and get some air with your dad."

Gabe knew an order when he heard one and obediently stood, kissed Johnny on his forehead, and walked toward his father, who was holding two takeout coffees. Before he reached his dad, Ellen opened her arms wide, giving Gabe the type of hug a mom gives when they know their son is about to get some bad news. Gabe couldn't help but wonder what else could possibly be wrong compared to the rest of the day.

Pulling away from his mom, Gabe looked into her eyes, hoping for some kind of clue as to what was happening. "Love you, son. Now go with your father, Gabe." *Shit, it's bad.*

With one last look at Johnny, he took the much-appreciated caffeine and followed his dad out into the front courtyard of the hospital. It was late and the night was quiet. Gabe and the chief walked in silence for a few minutes, and Gabe had the feeling his dad was trying to figure out how to say something.

"Why don't we have a seat?" Roger pointed toward a concrete bench and waited until they were both seated to begin. "They caught up with Chris just outside Brighton. There was nothing that could have been done."

"What do you mean, Dad? Is anyone else hurt?" Gabe wasn't sure what he would do if he found out someone else had been hurt by this madman; he'd had enough.

"Chris wouldn't surrender and was firing on nearby officers," Dad explained, his lip curled back in disgust for what Chris had done.

"Oh, my God, did he shoot someone?" *Christ, how has everything gotten so out of control?*

"No, but Chris is dead, Gabe. Spider had no other choice; he had to protect the other officers."

Gabe sat motionless, breathing deeply to keep the coffee he just drank inside his rolling stomach. He'd wanted Chris stopped, but he certainly didn't want him to die, even after threatening it himself in the heat of anger. After everything Chris had put them through, Gabe still believed most of the violence was brought out due to his drug use; the man had needed help. Even after the years spent with Chris and the love he had thought they shared, Gabe couldn't honestly say he felt the grief he should feel for the loss of someone he once loved. Was that wrong? He did feel the grief for the loss of life, as Gabe spent his own life saving others, but beyond that was only relief, which brought on its own sort of guilt.

"Don't think for one minute that any of this is your fault, son, or any guilt for feeling some sort of relief that this is finally over and your family is now safe. You didn't cause this. Chris's own greed and addiction is at fault, and he is responsible for his own death, no one else."

As Johnny would say, family telepathy was apparently out in full force.

"I just never would have thought something like this could happen to us. Hell, my biggest concern months ago was whether I'd ever find someone I could trust again. Now Chris is dead and the man I want to spend the rest of my life with is lying in another hospital bed because of me." Before Gabe's dad could tell him yet again that it wasn't his fault, Gabe carried on. "I know, logically, you and everyone else are right. That I didn't cause any of this, but it will take time for my heart to feel free of all the pain this caused the people I love."

"I understand, son. The family is here for you and Johnny." Roger assured and placed his arm around Gabe to give him a reassuring hug.

"I'm lucky Johnny's still here after everything he's been through," Gabe admitted.

"That boy loves you. He's not going anywhere without you. That's the kind of love your mom and I have, and I treasure it for the gift it is every day. You remember that, son."

"I will, Dad."

"And make an honest man out of that boy sooner rather than later. Your mom wants a wedding to plan. That should keep the Mason women busy for a bit. See, win-win." The chief laughed deeply, but Gabe knew his dad loved his mom and all the Mason women, even if they drove the men nuts at times.

"My thoughts exactly." He would marry Johnny and start that family he had dreamt of for what seemed like forever.

Once everyone had left the hospital for the night, Gabe climbed onto Johnny's bed and gathered him into his arms. Johnny snuggled further into his spot with his face pressed into Gabe's neck before sighing contentedly and falling back to sleep. Gabe knew he was blessed; he'd been given this chance at happiness, and for that, he would be eternally grateful.

Chapter Ten

Two weeks later

Johnny wondered if a man could actually die from having blue balls, because if Gabe didn't give in soon, he just might find out. Hot make-out sessions, cold showers, and jacking off were just not cutting it anymore. His lungs had finally healed and Johnny could take a deep breath now without pain, but his burns were another story. Though half of his bandages were now gone, the scarring was extensive on his hands, shoulder, and chest. His skin in these areas now had an almost waxy, white color with a raised, leathery texture that seemed almost tight. Honestly, Johnny wasn't sure how he felt about his scars, but he would move past them somehow and he would start today.

The brilliant sun peeked in and out from behind the many clouds on this beautiful July day. Family and friends were over at Gabe and Johnny's house, and yes, Johnny finally accepted the fact that he was never leaving and was in the process of subletting his old apartment. He and Gabe had only been together a few months, but the love he felt for that man was immeasurable. They would spend days together when Gabe wasn't working, just talking while Gabe held him in his chair in their beautiful greenhouse. For the longest while, that was all Johnny physically could do anyway, so it gave the two of them the time they needed to really learn about each other—which was wonderful really, but Johnny wanted sex now! Having his very own hot, muscled firefighter around had switched his libido from a slow simmer to the "find any flat surface" category.

Johnny watched the wonderful Mason women fluttering around the backyard, fussing over the children and setting out numerous containers of food that they always insisted on bringing. They had taken Johnny under their collective wings and he finally uncovered the reason why Aunt Casey was never allowed in the state of Kentucky again. You had to love the aunts.

Royce and Jesse had moved in to Royce's house as soon as Jesse was able to get around with his walker. Johnny still went and checked in on him every day, and they had become close friends since the accident. Jesse stood under a tree holding onto his walker with Royce by his side while talking to Spider, Dante, and Sam. Sam had recovered but still walked with a cane. Spider and Dante had yet to make plans to leave Brighton and return to their homes, causing Johnny to wonder how much of that decision depended on Sam. Gabe was working through his own feelings of guilt in the aftermath of Chris's death. Therefore, along with Johnny, they were both seeing a therapist weekly. It would take time, but Johnny had no doubt they would both come out of this stronger, further cementing their bond.

Johnny slowly made his way toward Gabe, watching as he laughed and talked with the chief and his brothers-in-law. He had noticed the shadows slowly disappearing from Gabe's eyes over the weeks. Johnny imagined pain like that would take a long time to put behind you, but he would be there for his love, and Gabe knew it.

"Hey, babe, having fun?" Gabe opened his arms wide as he always did for him and Johnny walked right into his embrace. "How are your hands? You've been doing a lot of cooking today. Do you think it's time for you to take a break?"

Johnny knew Gabe was just looking out for him, but Johnny had to start moving people past the damage to his hands so that they wouldn't feel the need to worry about them—or worry about offending him by mentioning the scars, which nobody spoke about. Absolutely *nobody*.

Ah, Kate's husband, Dave, Brighton's very own police chief, would be the perfect accomplice in his master plan. "Dave, can I ask you a professional question?"

Dave looked shocked at Johnny's formal tone but answered anyway. "You can ask me anything, Johnny; we're family." Johnny noticed the rest of their family and friends were taking interest in the conversation and Gabe just look confused.

Perfect.

Johnny attempted to look as innocent as possible before asking with a straight face. "So, will I be able to get away with a crime now that I don't have fingerprints?"

Dave shifted his weight from foot to foot and continued to stare at him, clearly uneasy and unsure where to go with the touchy subject of Johnny's scars. *Well, the sooner everyone gets over this, the sooner I might get laid.*

So Johnny pushed on. "Oh, don't worry, Dave. I'm not talking about murder or anything. Maybe just a little B&E on the side, you know, to supplement my income since I'm still not working full time."

A few of the gathered men's mouths opened as if to say something and then closed again like fish out of water. It wasn't until Grandma Rose and Mom started laughing that Johnny finally lost it and broke into laughter of his own.

The men slowly began to clue in when all the women were almost rolling on the ground and gave in to their own laughter.

"Well, Johnny, I would advise you not to do anything in the county 'cause I know those hands and I'll bust you anyway." Dave chuckled before taking a swig of his beer.

"Damn, you mean I don't get a family pass? Well, that just sucks." Johnny pouted before he began laughing right along with everyone else.

Once his family and friends had finally settled down, Johnny looked around at the people who filled his new life with joy and love. He became serious, which was odd for him, but it needed to be done. The "let's not mention his scars" time was over.

"I love this family. I love Gabe and all of you, but these"— Johnny thrust his hands out palms up so everyone could get a perfect view of the bandages and gnarled, white leathery flesh that covered the palms of his hands—"are just scars, and worrying about offending me by talking about them or worrying that I'm traumatized by them isn't necessary. Yes, I'm getting used to them, and yes, I'm learning how to use my fine motor skills again with the nerve damage. But I'm okay with that and whatever else I have to do because Josie and Janice are alive and Ben has his mother. Anything after that is just gravy anyway."

Gabe wrapped his muscled arms around Johnny and lifted him until he was at least a foot off the ground and they were face to face.

"You're absolutely right, Johnny. You've shown repeatedly how brave and strong you are. We should have known this wouldn't get in your way. I love you so much, baby."

"I love you too, big guy. Now that we have that out of the way, are you absolutely positive, Dave? Not just one family pass?" The family continued to chuckle and Gabe lowered Johnny back to the ground.

Johnny turned to walk toward the picnic tables until he heard Frannie gasp and spun around to face Gabe who was now down on one knee with a black velvet box in his hand. Gabe opened the box with shaking hands, and Johnny was amazed he was still able to stand when he saw the beautiful bands inside. Two square, princess-cut diamonds sparkled in the sunlight and were surrounded by etched flames. They were simply stunning.

"Gabe—?"

"Johnny, there's no one else I would ever want to spend my life with." Gabe stood up and pulled Johnny into his arms. "I thought I knew what love felt like, but I had no idea, not until you came into my life. You've brought me so much joy and happiness; you own me. I can't live without you." Gabe's eyes became impossibly darker as he stared down at Johnny. "Will you spend the rest of your life with me—will you marry me and have a family with me?"

Johnny could feel his heart trying to beat its way out of his chest. Everything he had ever dreamed of was wrapped up in this amazing man, and that man wanted to marry him. How had he gotten this lucky?

"Yes." It was as simple as that, and the only word he could say before Gabe slammed his mouth over his in a devastating kiss that rocked him down to his toes. Johnny's life had been filled with feelings of inadequacy and loneliness until the day his life was saved, in more ways than one, by this courageous fireman. As Gabe carefully slid the symbol of their love on Johnny's finger and he did the same to Gabe, Johnny knew he was finally home.

Cheering and congratulations finally filtered through their bubble of happiness as the family swooped in. Plans were made, and the Mason women went into complete wedding mode. Mercifully, Gabe and Johnny would simply have to show up and nothing more according to the women. Johnny just knew he wasn't going to get off that easily. Still had to love those Mason women.

Hours later, with dishes washed and family and friends gone to their respective homes, Johnny found himself pressed against the living room wall, moaning loudly as Gabe mapped his mouth with his tongue. His hunger for Gabe drove his lust to unimaginable levels. Johnny needed the fabric between them gone, *now*. Gabe's thigh pushed between Johnny's legs, allowing him to grind his aching cock against it, desperate for relief.

Gabe pulled away and looked at Johnny through lust-hazed eyes. "Babe, I need you. I need to be deep inside you. I don't know how gentle I can be right now. That's why I've been trying to wait. I'm having a hard time controlling myself."

"Need…now." Johnny was so turned on that he was reduced to single words. His brain had shut down, caught in a haze of sensations and the driving need to feel the man in his arms fuck him into the mattress or the wall—or the couch; Johnny wasn't picky.

Apparently, that was all the permission Gabe needed. The sound of ripping material and buttons tinkling to the ground barely registered. His pants were next as Gabe's pace became frantic. Soon Johnny found himself and Gabe naked, wrapped around each other and pressed back against that same wall. Gabe's lips were rough, demanding, and driving Johnny closer to the edge by the second. He was all for making love right here, but it seemed his lover had other plans.

Gabe lifted him up higher while Johnny wrapped himself around Gabe and continued to explore his soon-to-be husband's mouth. It wasn't until his back landed on the soft blankets of their bed that Johnny broke the kiss. Gabe's eyes shone with all the love Johnny had wished for his entire life; this brave, compassionate man gave Johnny exactly what he needed. Gabe saw Johnny; he never looked through him, and he never thought less of him. He was Gabe's equal and he was loved.

"I love you, Johnny." Gabe's voice wavered slightly with emotion, but he pushed on. "You're everything to me."

Johnny's breath caught in his lungs. He had never been everything to anyone. He had spent his entire life as someone with little to no value to his father. Now he had everything. Gabe gave that to him.

"I love you more than I can explain, Gabe." It was true. Johnny knew Gabe would never fully grasp what he'd given to him, but

Johnny would make sure to show him every day for the rest of their lives.

Gabe growled, lowered his head, and took Johnny's cock all the way to the root inside his warm, wet mouth, tearing a cry of sheer ecstasy from Johnny. Gabe hollowed his cheeks, the suction sending tingles down his spine and causing Johnny to buck his hips further into Gabe's talented mouth. All coherent thought fled when he began to swirl his tongue around Johnny's sensitive glans; he was going to come soon if Gabe didn't stop.

"Going to...come..." Johnny panted desperately, pumping his hips upward.

Gabe immediately pulled off his cock with one last lick. "Not until I'm balls deep inside you, Johnny."

Gabe reached into the bedside table and pulled out a bottle of lube. Johnny was so desperate for Gabe's touch that he pulled his legs up to his chest to give Gabe better access.

"You're so beautiful," Gabe murmured before pushing one lubed finger into his waiting hole in a slow, maddening pace.

Johnny inhaled sharply and pushed back, that little bit of pain morphing into pleasure within moments, making him groan and pant. Gabe wasn't wasting any time. As soon as Johnny's body became accustomed to the invasion, he added another finger and then another. Johnny was delirious as wave after wave of pleasure raced through his body. He massaged Johnny's prostate with his talented fingers and Johnny swore, if it hadn't been for Gabe's hand on his hip, he would have shot straight off the bed. Johnny's cock was leaving trails of precum all over his stomach as he lay writhing under Gabe's capable hands.

"Gabe...please, I need you." Johnny wasn't above begging at this point.

Gabe pulled his fingers from Johnny, leaving him feeling empty for only a moment before he felt the blunt head of Gabe's cock at his entrance. Blood tests weeks ago confirmed no need for condoms. "Push out, Johnny."

Johnny knew it had been a long while since he had been with anyone, and other than Gabe's fingers, they hadn't made love yet, so the stretch and burn were no surprise. He pushed out and tried to relax as much as he could with what felt like a two-by-four trying to split him in half. Johnny didn't care; he simply needed Gabe inside him. Slowly, inch by glorious inch, Gabe slid into him until his balls rested against Johnny's ass.

Gabe hovered only mere inches from Johnny's face, holding most of his weight on his arms. The beads of sweat on his forehead were tribute to how much control Gabe was using in trying not to move and allowing Johnny time to adjust to his invasion.

Johnny had other ideas. Lifting his hips slightly, he began to impale himself on Gabe's rock-hard cock, desperate for relief. It seemed that was all the incentive Gabe needed. He pulled back so that only the head was still inside Johnny's ass before slamming back in. Johnny cried out in pleasure, meeting him thrust for thrust as Gabe set a desperate pace, his eyes never leaving Johnny's.

Johnny was panting and begging for more. Reaching between them, he grabbed his own leaking cock, needing more friction as he drove toward his own release. Johnny's actions seemed to spur Gabe on. The bed creaked and slammed against the bedroom wall, but Johnny didn't care in the least; all that mattered was him and Gabe. In that moment, the world drifted away and it was only the two of them. Their desire and love drove them higher and higher.

Gabe's movements became even more erratic as he pegged Johnny's hot spot over and over until the tingling in Johnny's spine spread, drawing his balls up tight. Johnny cried out as he shot cum over his and Gabe's stomachs. That was all it took to set Gabe off. His cock swelled, stretching Johnny even wider before he roared his release, filling Johnny with his hot cum. Moments later, Gabe collapsed on top of him, but Johnny figured that since he could still breathe that Gabe must still be aware enough to be holding most of his weight off of him. Without even pulling himself out, Gabe rolled the two of them over until Johnny was lying on top of him. The events of the day must have caught up with Johnny, because the next thing he felt was a warm cloth between his cheeks cleaning him. He hadn't even realized Gabe had lifted him off his chest or that he had gone to the washroom to get items to care for him.

"I can do that," Johnny mumbled into the pillow, not entirely sure if he liked being taken care of this way.

"I've got you, baby. Please let me take care of you." Gabe spoke softly, taking the fight right out of Johnny. He knew Gabe was a nurturer and the dominate one in this relationship, and Johnny was perfectly happy with that.

A few moments later, Gabe crawled back onto the bed beside Johnny and gathered him into his strong arms before pulling the blanket over the both of them and settling in for the night.

"Thank you." Gabe whispered so softly that Johnny barely heard him. He lifted his head to look at Gabe curiously.

"Thank you for what, big guy?"

Gabe smiled at him, and the love shining in his eyes made Johnny feel invincible. "I thought you were asleep, baby. That wasn't for you. I was thanking fate for bringing you to me." Gabe finished by kissing the ring on Johnny's finger.

A wave of love washed over Johnny. This amazing man was thankful to simply have Johnny just the way he was. There had to be someone looking out for Johnny the day of that office fire. In his heart, he wanted to believe it had been his dear mother, and he swore to her that he would never squander what he'd been given.

"Love you to the moon, Gabe."

"Yes, to the moon, Johnny."

The End

ABOUT THE AUTHOR

M. Tasia is a paralegal and author who lives in Ontario, Canada. She's a member of the RWA and its chapter RRW. She's a dedicated people watcher, and a lover of romance, '80s rock, and happy endings. She's also the mother of two wonderful girls and a servant to two spoiled furry children.

Did you enjoy this book? Drop us a line and say so! We love to hear from readers, and so do our authors. To connect, visit www.boroughspublishinggroup.com online, send comments directly to info@boroughspublishinggroup.com, or friend us on Facebook and Twitter. And be sure to check back regularly for contests and new releases in your favorite subgenres of romance!

Are you an aspiring writer? Check out www.boroughspublishinggroup.com/submit and see if we can help you make your dreams come true.

63478689R00063

Made in the USA
Charleston, SC
04 November 2016